The Mystery of the Invisible Knight

Bethany House Books by
Bill Myers

Journeys to Fayrah
CHILDREN'S ALLEGORICAL SERIES

> *The Portal*
> *The Experiment*
> *The Whirlwind*
> *The Tablet*

Bloodhounds, Inc.
CHILDREN'S MYSTERY SERIES

> *The Ghost of KRZY*
> *The Mystery of the Invisible Knight*
> *Phantom of the Haunted Church*
> *Invasion of the UFOs*
> *Fangs for the Memories*
> *The Case of the Missing Minds*

Nonfiction

> *The Dark Side of the Supernatural*
> *Hot Topics, Tough Questions*

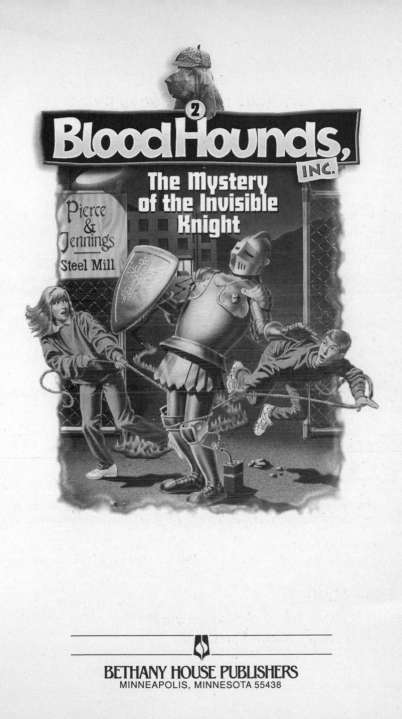

BloodHounds, INC. ②

The Mystery of the Invisible Knight

Pierce & Jennings Steel Mill

BETHANY HOUSE PUBLISHERS
MINNEAPOLIS, MINNESOTA 55438

Published by Bethany House Publishers
A Ministry of Bethany Fellowship International
11400 Hampshire Avenue South
Minneapolis, Minnesota 55438
www.bethanyhouse.com

Printed in the United States of America by
Bethany Press International, Minneapolis, Minnesota 55438

Library of Congress Cataloging-in-Publication Data

Myers, Bill, 1953–
    The mystery of the invisible knight / by Bill Myers.
       p. cm. — (Bloodhounds, Inc. ; 2)
    Summary: Sean and Misty learn not to be afraid when God is on their side as they investigate a string of robberies in which the only suspect is an invisible knight.
    ISBN 1-55661-891-3 (pbk.)
    [1. Brothers and sisters—Fiction. 2. Christian life—Fiction. 3. Mystery and detective stories.] I. Title. II. Series: Myers, Bill,
1953–   Bloodhounds, Inc. ; 2.
PZ7.M98234Ip   1997
[Fic]—dc21   97-21043
                                                  CIP
                                                  AC

For **Jeanne Mikkelson,**

*a godly woman
of wisdom and commitment.*

BILL MYERS is a youth worker and a creative writer and film director who co-created the "McGee and Me!" book and video series and whose work has received over forty national and international awards. His many youth books include THE INCREDIBLE WORLDS OF WALLY MCDOOGLE, JOURNEYS TO FAYRAH, as well as his teen books, *Hot Topics, Tough Questions* and *Forbidden Doors*. He also writes and acts for Focus on the Family's *Odyssey* radio series.

Contents

Don't be afraid, for I have ransomed you;
I have called you by name; you are mine.
When you go through deep waters
and great trouble, I will be with you.
When you go through rivers of difficulty,
you will not drown!
When you walk through the fire of oppression,
you will not be burned up
—the flames will not consume you.
For I am the Lord your God, your Savior,
the Holy One of Israel.

ISAIAH 43:1–3, TLB

1

The Case Begins

The alley was dark.

Real dark.

Not dark like the garage when you can't find the light and wonder if the shadow over there is the rake or really a monster waiting to eat you. And not dark like your grandma's cellar when she asks you to go down and get a can of peas. (Thanks, Grandma, I just love risking my life for a green vegetable.) No, I mean dark like being a blind man in a dark room looking for a black cat that isn't there. That kind of dark. In other words . . .

It was kinda hard to see.

That's exactly what Mr. Morrisey was thinking as he stepped out of his jewelry shop and into the back alley. Once again the streetlight had burned out, which meant he had to fumble with his keys to lock the back door. But that was okay because he'd soon be home eating a delicious plate of overcooked cauliflower and broccoli while watching a *Gilligan's Island* rerun. He'd then top off this incredibly exciting evening by soaking his dentures. (Does this guy know how to have fun or what?)

But tonight . . . tonight would be just a little different because—

Clank.

The loud, metallic sound echoed through the alley. Mr. Morrisey's heart skipped a beat.

Clank. Clank.

Mr. Morrisey's heart skipped two beats.

The sound was closer . . . and quickly approaching. The old man thought of running. But at his age, he'd be lucky to outrun a dead turtle. And the best he could make out, this was no turtle.

"Who . . . who's there?" he called.

Clank.

"I said, who's—"

Clank. Clank.

Now Mr. Morrisey could finally make out a shape. A

very large shape. He began to back away.

Clank! Clank! Clank!

Slowly, it emerged into a faint pool of light. Now Morrisey could see it clearly. It was a knight! From the days of King Arthur. And even in the dimness, its suit of armor seemed to glow.

Mr. Morrisey continued backing away as the knight continued closing in, its metal armor crashing with every step.

Clank! Clank! Clank!

Suddenly the thing came to a stop.

The old jeweler stood watching, shaking like a plate of Jell-O on a jackhammer, as the knight slowly raised its arm. Then even more slowly, it lifted the face visor of its helmet to reveal . . .

Nothing!

That's right, it was completely empty—as in the visor was open, but nobody was home!

Mr. Morrisey could take no more. He fainted. Just like that. Out cold. Not dead, but not waking up for a while, either.

The knight calmly closed its helmet and turned back toward the open door of the jewelry store.

FRIDAY 11: 49 PDST

The next morning Sean and Melissa Hunter, along with their faithful bloodhound, Slobs, were visiting Doc in her creaky old house. They were up in her creaky old laboratory, sitting on an even creakier old sofa.

At the moment Doc was carefully applying a thick brown paste to a long, cone-shaped gizmo that was hooked up to some sort of thingamabob that was wired to a bunch of fancy doodads and diodes. In short, it looked exactly like something Doc would invent . . . which meant it was probably something that would be blowing up.

But that didn't stop Doc any. No, sir. She plugged it in.

Mistake Number One.

Then she turned the cone toward the window and flipped on the switch.

Mistake Number Two.

Suddenly there was a tremendous FLASH, followed by some rather usual

> *Whistlings* . . .
> *Whizzings* . . .
> and *Bangings!*

Having seen Doc's experiments at work before,

everyone did what they always did when she turned them on . . . they screamed and ran for cover. Misty and Sean leaped under a nearby table, and Slobs pushed until she got her head under a sofa cushion.

The machine began to shake and shudder, growing louder and louder. Any second now and the whole thing would blow up. Any second now and they'd be vaporized into a gigantic mushroom cloud that—

PSSSSSSssssssssss . . .

That was it. No explosion. No thermonuclear meltdown. Just a loud hiss that slowly faded until the machine fell silent.

Sean and Melissa glanced at each other and sighed in relief.

Doc shook her head, grabbed a screwdriver, and went back to work.

By now you've probably figured out Doc is a woman. If you didn't, don't feel bad. It's hard to tell with her thick hair, huge black spectacles, and baggy lab coat. And you certainly couldn't tell by listening to her talk. The reason was simple:

She didn't.

Well, not much. Doc was born deaf. But don't feel sorry for her. She could do more than a dozen people who could hear put together. Somehow the silence allowed her to concentrate harder on her inventions . . . like Jeremiah over there. . . .

"Let's try it again!" the redheaded, 3-D cartoon creature called from inside a computer monitor. "If at first you don't succeed, cry, cry again!"

Good old Jeremiah. He was some sort of computer intelligence that Doc had created nearly six months ago. (Although "intelligence" might be a bit of an exaggeration when it came to Jeremiah.) It's not that he was stupid, it's just that the only reality he'd ever experienced was inside the TV screens, computer monitors, and digital watches where he lived.

Even that would have been okay . . . except for his little run-in with the fortune cookie factory. It seems one day he had traveled downline, accidentally entered the factory's computer, and downloaded himself with a gazillion proverbs and catchy old sayings. Unfortunately, his circuitry had majorly overloaded, so although he had learned every proverb and saying, they were all mixed up and garbled.

"Let's try again," he shouted. "A stitch in time saves nine lives!"

See what I mean?

As he spoke, the words formed on the bottom of a nearby screen so Doc could read them. She nodded and reached over to the switch for another try.

Sean threw Melissa a look. "Uh-oh," he groaned, "here we go again!"

Before they could duck for cover (or at least buy a good life insurance policy), Doc flipped the switch.

But this time there was no flash. That was good news. Neither were there any *whistlings, whizzings,* or *bangings.* More good news.

Unfortunately, there was a little bad

BOINNG-OING-OING-OING-OING-OING-OING. . . .

The noise was deafening, filling the room and going on forever. And just when you thought forever had come and gone, it went on a little longer.

Sean and Melissa covered their ears. Poor Slobs howled and bayed. Even little Jeremiah was in pain as his face turned every color of the rainbow (cartoon characters can do that). Of course, Doc didn't hear a thing and kept working . . . until she turned around and saw their expressions. Then she reached down and immediately pulled the plug.

The noise slowly faded.

. . . OING-OING-Oing-Oing-oing-oing-oing

"What was that?" Melissa cried.

Sean would have asked, too, but he was busy sticking

his finger in his ear, shaking out any excess *BOINGs* still rattling around in there.

"That's the Age Detector," Jeremiah chirped. "All you have to do is smear that paste over the cone, turn it on, and point it at something to learn its age."

"Is it supposed to be that noisy?" Sean asked.

Jeremiah nodded. "Sure. Each *BOING* represents one year."

As the two talked, Melissa crossed toward the window.

"But those *BOINGs* went on forever," Sean complained. "What was she pointing at?"

"I think I might have an answer," Melissa called.

They turned to her.

"Wasn't she pointing it out this window?"

Sean moved closer. "But at what?"

They turned to Doc. The woman was already typing her explanation into the computer:

"I WAS AIMING FOR THAT TREE, BUT MISSED
AND HIT THE SUN. UNFORTUNATELY, THE
SUN'S A LITTLE TOO OLD . . . WHICH MEANS
A FEW TOO MANY *BOINGS*. SORRY."

Sean and Melissa looked at each other and sighed. Once again Doc had almost made an incredible breakthrough. But "almost" was as close as she ever seemed to get. Like Jeremiah and everything else she invented, there was always a minor little problem—a minor little problem that usually led to a major catastrophe.

Suddenly they were interrupted by another sound—the squealing and squawking from a nearby radio. They turned to the stereo and saw Jeremiah inside the digital tuner, pushing and pulling at the numbers.

"Jeremiah," Sean called, "what are you doing?"

"It's show time," the little guy cried as he continued to push and kick at the digital numbers until they hit the right frequency. "Time for your dad's newscast."

" . . . big story in Middleton today." Their father's voice came in loud and clear. "Seems there was a mysterious robbery at Morrisey Jewelers."

The word "mysterious" definitely perked up Sean's and Melissa's ears.

"Mr. Morrisey was found unconscious at the rear entrance to his store last night. When he awoke, he claimed the place had been robbed by a . . . get this now . . . he claimed the place had been robbed by a *knight* dressed in full armor."

"Did you hear that?" asked Sean.

Melissa nodded. "A knight."

"In full armor."

"Sean, you're not thinking—"

17

"You bet I am." He beamed. "Sounds like another case for Bloodhounds, Inc."

"I don't know," she said reluctantly. "If you ask me, I think—"

"Come on, let's go!" He turned and started toward the door.

Melissa was never sure how Sean had talked her into forming the private detective agency. Unlike her brother, who loved any kind of adventure (as long as it didn't require a whole lot of thinking), Misty's idea of excitement was curling up with a cup of hot chocolate and reading about it in a book. But as the older of the two (by a whole eleven months), Sean had been able to wear her down until he'd finally gotten his way. (Older brothers are good at that sort of thing.)

So now, thanks to Mr. Morrisey's break-in, the stolen jewels, and a mysterious knight, it looked like they were about to start another adventure.

The two said quick good-byes to Doc and Jeremiah, then headed down the stairs with Slobs hot on their heels. Another case was about to begin. . . .

2

Sandwich to Go!

FRIDAY 12:13 PDST

Herbie, the balding radio engineer, sat with his feet propped up on the control counsel. He was eating a gigantic ham, tuna, cheese, dill pickle, and whatever-else-was-left-in-the-station's-refrigerator sandwich. In front of him, through the glass window, sat his boss, Sean and Melissa's dad. Mr. Hunter was inside the broadcast booth, wrapping up the newscast.

Herbie carefully balanced the sandwich in one hand and leaned over to adjust the volume control with the other. That's when Sean, Melissa, and Slobs burst into the room, causing him to fall off his chair, fling his sandwich against the booth's window, and peg the volume control all the way into the red.

Feedback squealed through the speakers and across

the airwaves of KRZY Radio.

"What do you think you're doing!" Herbie shouted as he scrambled to his feet. "You can't come in and ruin your dad's . . . your dad's . . . uh-oh . . ."

The yelling was because he was mad. The "uh-oh" was because Dad was glaring at him through the glass and pointing to Herbie's mike switch. Apparently, ol' Herb had bumped into it during his fall. No biggie, except it meant that he'd turned it on and the entire town had just heard his little yelling performance.

Dad looked steamed—though it was pretty hard to tell through the glass covered in mayonnaise, ham, slices of dill pickle, and globs of tuna fish . . . all slowly oozing to the floor. He turned back to his mike and did his best to save the newscast. "Well, that's the news in Middleton. My name is Robert Hunter, and those other sounds were, of course, my children dropping by to visit."

Sean and Melissa exchanged sheepish looks.

Dad continued. "Now it's back to music with the Dueling Accordions, playing their rendition of 'Macarena.' "

As the music came up, Dad took off his headphones and slowly opened the broadcast booth door. He was definitely not smiling.

"Uh-oh," Sean groaned under his breath.

"Ditto," Melissa whispered.

Herbie, wanting to keep his job a little longer, decided to retreat to the back room to grab some rags and glass cleaner.

Everything was deathly silent . . . except for Slobs, who was standing on her back legs, slurping, licking, and gobbling down as much of the window delicacy as she could reach.

"Uh, hi, Dad," Melissa said, trying to grin.

Dad looked at her. When he spoke, his voice was very low and very stern. "Hello, guys . . ." But no matter how hard he tried, he could never stay angry at them—not for long. He finally broke into a reluctant smile and finished. ". . . and hello trouble."

Melissa and Sean sighed in relief. They knew he could tell it had been an accident.

Herbie returned with the glass cleaner and began a race with Slobs to clean the glass as Dad patiently answered his kids' questions about the robbery.

"What exactly happened?" Sean asked.

"Remember all those suits of armor at the museum?" Dad said.

"Sure." Melissa nodded. "Downstairs in the medieval section."

"Well, it turns out there's a legend about one of them."

"A legend?" Sean said.

"Which one?" Melissa asked. "What type of legend?"

"It's the armor belonging to a Sir Richard Falcrest. The legend claims that one day he would return from the dead and avenge the loss of his castle."

"Return from the dead." Melissa swallowed. "You don't think he could really do such a thing?"

"Don't be ignorant," Sean scorned. "Of course he couldn't." Then turning back to Dad, he asked, "Could he?"

Dad smiled. "We've talked about this before. The Bible says that once we die, we go and stand before God in judgment. No stopping off and haunting houses or scaring people along the way."

"So you don't think it's a ghost?" Melissa asked.

"No. And even if it were something weird or supernatural, you still wouldn't have to be afraid."

"We wouldn't?" Sean asked.

"You've got God on your side . . . remember?"

"Oh yeah."

Melissa also nodded. And for the most part she believed him. Still, there was that small part deep inside that wasn't so sure.

"What else?" Sean asked. "About the robbery, I mean."

"Well . . ." Dad reached into his pocket. "I got this off

the wire service. It's a note left at the jewelry store after the robbery."

"What's it say?" they both asked in unison.

Dad unfolded the paper. "The police found it this morning. It reads:

'I have taken the rubies from your store
to adorn my sword. I will need gold
for its handle and your finest steel to
forge the blade. When that is accomplished,
I will unleash my curse upon your city,
upon all descendants of those who
overthrew my kingdom.' "

Sean whistled. Melissa tried to swallow, but her mouth was bone dry.

"So the knight stole a bunch of rubies?" Sean asked.

"That's right," Dad answered. "Nothing else, just rubies—supposedly to decorate its sword."

"How weird."

"But it doesn't sound like it's quite finished," Melissa said, finally finding her voice.

"What do you mean?"

She pointed at the note. "It says it still needs gold for the handle and steel for the blade."

"You're right." Sean nodded. "So it might strike again."

"This could get serious," Dad said.

Sean nodded even more eagerly. "I'll say!"

Dad continued, "Serious enough that I hope you two will keep your noses out of it."

"It could just be a prank," Melissa offered.

Dad shrugged. "Prank or not, it sounds like Mr. Morrisey was in danger, and if you ask me—"

"We know, Dad." Sean sighed. He then recited the lecture he and Melissa had heard a dozen times. " 'This is adult stuff, and the police should handle it.' "

"That's right," Dad agreed.

"And they will," Sean insisted. "But we're a private detective agency. It's our job to look into this sort of thing. Isn't that right, Misty?"

Melissa, who appeared anything but excited, knew she was supposed to agree, so she gave a reluctant nod. "Yeah . . . sure."

"Besides," Sean turned back to Dad, "you knew there would be dangers when you let us start Bloodhounds, Inc."

Dad took a deep breath and slowly let it out. "All right, I see your point. But be smart, okay? And if you stumble on something, be sure to bring in the police."

"You bet!" Sean agreed enthusiastically.

"Yeah . . . sure," Melissa repeated, not quite so enthusiastically.

"Now," Dad started back into the broadcast booth, "I've got a commercial coming up. Did you do the list of chores I left on the counter?"

"Sure." Sean nodded.

Melissa shot him a look.

"Uh . . . I mean some of them," Sean hedged.

She gave him another look. "Well, we were *thinking* about doing them."

"See to it that you do *all of them*," Dad said. "With Mom gone we've all got to pull our weight around here."

Sean and Melissa nodded slowly. It had been six months since Mom had died, and they were still adjusting. At times the pain was so heavy in their chests that if made it almost impossible to breathe. At other times it felt like she was away on some trip and would be coming home any day.

But of course she never did.

After saying good-bye to Dad, they headed for the door. Unfortunately, it was the same door that Herbie had chosen to reenter with a remake of his ham, tuna, and everything sandwich.

Not only was it the same door, but it was the same time.

Once again Herbie crashed to the floor, and once again his prized sandwich went airborne until it hit—you guessed it—the broadcast booth's window . . . smearing it with sandwich parts and mayo.

FRIDAY, 12:55 PDST

"Soon as we get these chores done," Sean said, "we'll head down to the museum and check out the exhibit on that Sir Richard Falcrest guy."

"I doubt we'll have time today," Melissa said as she looked over the list Dad had left on the kitchen counter.

"Why not?"

"See for yourself."

Sean grabbed the list and read:

Mop floor
Wash and dry laundry
Dust blinds
Do dishes
Mow lawn

"Wonderful . . ." he groaned. "We'll be here forever."

With any luck, Melissa hoped that's exactly where they would be. It's not that she was afraid of this particular case. She just wished that their agency would spend a little more time finding cute kittens caught in trees and a little less time tracking down angry medieval ghosts.

At least for today it looked like she'd get her wish . . . until she heard that all too familiar squeaky little voice.

"Hey, guys, what's baking?"

She gave a start, then looked around the kitchen. Of course she knew it was Jeremiah, and of course she knew he meant, "What's cooking?" but at the moment she couldn't find him anywhere. It was Sean who finally spotted him . . . in the clock of the microwave.

"Hey, Jeremiah," he called. "We've got a ton of housework to do. Got any ideas on how we can get it done faster?"

"No problem-o," Jeremiah chirped. "My memory banks have recorded every *Brady Bunch, Leave It to Beaver,* and *I Love Lucy* rerun ever made."

"Meaning?"

"Meaning if they don't have an answer, who does?"

Sean nodded his head thoughtfully.

Melissa hesitated. "I don't know . . ."

"Don't be such a worry callous," Jeremiah squeaked. "Just follow my plans, and we'll be done lickety-spit."

"I think you mean worry *wart*," Melissa corrected. "And the term is lickety-*split*, not *spit*."

"Good point," Jeremiah agreed. "That will keep things a lot more sanitary."

Melissa rolled her eyes. Sometimes working with six-month-old computer creatures can get on your nerves.

"Let's hear what you've got!" Sean exclaimed.

Melissa rolled her eyes again. Sometimes working with older brothers can *really* get on your nerves.

Jeremiah quickly ran through his memory banks, and in a matter of seconds he had the answers.

First there was the floor.

"Just water it down and squirt soap on it," Jeremiah suggested. "Then tie sponges to Slobs' feet and turn her loose."

"Are you sure that will work?" Sean asked.

"Absolutely. I saw it on some Saturday morning cartoon."

His solution for washing the clothes wasn't much better. Before Melissa could stop him, Sean had agreed to put all of their dirty clothes into the tub and fill it with soap and water. Now the two of them were jumping up and down on the clothes, squishing and squirting the water in every direction.

"Isn't this cool?" Sean shouted to her. "This way we can get them all done in one load."

"But what about drying them?" Melissa demanded.

Unfortunately, Jeremiah had a solution for that as well. In a matter of minutes every one of their ceiling fans had shirts, pants, socks, and underwear pinned to the blades, which spun around and around and around.

Mowing the lawn was no better. . . .

Jeremiah wasn't sure what show he'd seen this on. But since the mower was self-propelled, all Sean had to do was drive a stake in the middle of the yard, connect the mower to it with a rope, and let it go around the stake in tighter and tighter circles.

"A piece of pie!" Jeremiah chirped.

Finally, there were the Venetian blinds. Dusting them was always a chore. But not now. Not with the help of Clueless, their cat, and little Crash 'n' Burn, their hamster. "Just put Crash 'n' Burn on the top blind, where he's nice and safe," Jeremiah ordered. "Then tie a duster to Clueless's tail and let her go."

The rest, as they say, would be history. Clueless (who did not get her name by accident) would spend all afternoon running back and forth, jumping up and down, trying to reach little Crash 'n' Burn.

"By the time you get home." Jeremiah beamed. "The blinds will be completely dusted."

Sean nodded enthusiastically. "And the floor mopped and the lawn mowed and the clothes dried."

"You hit the nail on the foot," Jeremiah agreed.

Soon everything was set and they were heading for the door.

"Guys," Melissa protested, "don't you think we should stick around?"

"What for?"

"In case something goes wrong?"

"What could go wrong!" Sean exclaimed.

"That's right," Jeremiah agreed. He was now inside Melissa's digital watch, talking from her wrist. "We've got all our bases smothered."

Melissa could only shake her head. "Did you put soap in the dishwasher?" she asked.

"It's in and running," Sean called as he headed out the door. "Let's go."

Melissa gave a long sigh, then reluctantly followed them outside, onto their bikes, and off to the museum.

3

Sir Richard Falcrest

FRIDAY, 16:07 PDST

Sean and Melissa stood shivering in the basement of the Middleton Museum.

"Don't they ever heat this place?" Sean asked as he rubbed his hands together.

Melissa tired to ignore him. She knew if he didn't have something to complain about, he wouldn't be happy. That was his style. Some girls have brothers who are brains or artists or star athletes. Hers was a brother who would win a gold medal in the Olympics . . . just as soon as they created an event for bellyaching.

But Melissa was also shivering (though she doubted it had as much to do with the temperature as it did with the suit of armor looming in front of her). The two of them stood in the museum's Medieval Exhibit. It consisted mostly of a long row of suits of armor lined up from the stairs and running across the room. The one that towered over them, the armor of Sir Richard Falcrest, was separated from the others. It was by far the largest . . . and the most foreboding. It stood at attention on a platform with its shield fixed across its chest.

Melissa was the first to spot a wooden plaque on the stand at its feet. She stooped down and began to read out loud:

" 'Sir Richard Falcrest,
the Lord of Duffington,
was a cruel feudal lord. He taxed his people
unfairly and treated them so poorly that
eventually he was overthrown by his own
peasants.' "

"Nice guy," Sean said.

"There's more." She went on to read:

" 'It is believed that many of the citizens of
Middleton are direct descendants of these
very peasants and—' "

"Are you kidding?" Sean interrupted. His voice echoed loudly against the concrete walls. "It says that?" Melissa cringed at Sean's volume. She caught a glimpse of the museum's curator, Mr. Jennings. The short little man had been giving them the eye ever since they'd approached the exhibit. Now he was frowning at Sean's loudness.

But Sean didn't notice. He never noticed that sort of stuff. "Where?" he demanded even more loudly. "Show me where it says that."

Melissa pointed down to the plaque.

"That's incredible!" he cried.

Melissa threw another look over at the curator. She hadn't thought it possible, but the man's scowl had actually grown deeper.

Now Sean was shuffling over to the display case beside the armor. "Hey, check this out!" he shouted.

"What is it?" Melissa whispered, hoping her brother would take the hint.

(But of course he didn't.)

"It's the replica of Sir Richard's sword!" he cried.

Melissa crossed to join him. Sure enough, there inside the case was a model of a sword—the blade painted silver to look like steel, along with a fake gold handle embedded with cut red glass.

"Check out the fake jewels!" Sean exclaimed. "They're supposed to be rubies."

"So?"

"So rubies were exactly what the knight had set out

to steal. This proves it really *was* him."

"Why do you say that?" Melissa asked, swallowing back her rising fear.

Sean sighed his best Why-am-I-surrounded-by-such-ignorance? sigh. "If it were a regular burglar, he would have taken more stuff. Why didn't he steal other jewels or diamonds or bracelets and necklaces? Why did he take only what the knight needs to make his sword?"

Melissa looked back at the fake sword and fought off a shiver. "But that's impossible. He's been dead for hundreds of years."

"You tell him that."

"All right, kids." The curator's voice made them both jump. Mr. Jennings was crossing the room, jabbing his finger at them. "You are far too loud. I'm going to have to ask you to leave."

"We're sorry," Melissa said. "We didn't mean to be. We're just excited because we're detectives and—"

"Detectives!" the short little man scoffed. "You're just children."

But Sean barely heard the put-down. "Is this sword an exact replica of the one Sir Falcrest had?"

"That's what it says," Jennings growled.

"Of the one he's supposedly remaking?"

The curator seemed to grow just a little pale. "Who told you about that?"

"Our dad's Robert Hunter, the owner of KRZY," Melissa explained. "He read us the police report."

Jennings looked a little more nervous and a lot more frightened. "That's . . . that's just an old wives' tale," he shuddered. "Falcrest has been dead for over five hundred years. He couldn't possibly be alive. There's absolutely no way."

Brother and sister exchanged glances. "Okay," Sean said slowly, "then maybe you could you tell us something about the curse."

"Curse?" Jennings shifted even more nervously.

Sean nodded, keeping a careful eye on him. "Something about a curse on the descendants who overthrew his kingdom."

Melissa nodded and pointed at the plaque. "It says here he would come after the peasants' descendants and that many of them live right in this town."

Jennings glanced about nervously. "As I said, I think it's time for you two to go home."

"But we're just—"

"The museum is closing."

"Not yet," Melissa corrected. "We've got another five minutes—"

"We shut this exhibit down early," the curator snapped. "That way nobody gets locked down here by accident." He pressed his hands against both of their backs and ushered them toward the stairs. "And you would not want to get trapped down here at night, believe you me."

"Why not?" Sean asked, still trying to get more information.

"Trust me," Jennings said as he moved them up the steps. "You definitely don't want to be down here in the dark."

But Sean, who was always too curious for his own good (and for Melissa's), turned back to Mr. Jennings with one last question. Unfortunately, it never quite got asked. It seems Sean's foot did a little slipping off a step, which caused his body to do a lot of falling back into Melissa.

Not a big deal, except it sent Melissa falling back into Mr. Jennings.

Even that would have been okay if Mr. Jennings hadn't lost his balance and started tumbling, head over heels, down the stairs.

Melissa and Sean stared in disbelief. But the gymnastics weren't over yet. . . .

When Mr. Jennings finally landed at the bottom, he slammed into the nearest suit of armor. Everyone watched in horror as that armor creaked, then slowly tilted until it fell into the suit of armor beside it . . . which creaked and fell into the one beside it, which creaked and fell into the—well, you probably get the picture.

creeeaak . . . CRASH!
creeeaak . . . CRASH!
creeeaak . . . CRASH!

On and on it went. Like a giant game of steel dominoes, one suit toppling into another. When they had finally finished and the dust had settled, only Sir Richard Falcrest's armor, which stood out by itself, remained on its feet. Everything else lay in a scattered heap across the floor.

Mr. Jennings rose, trembling in rage. He slowly turned toward Melissa and Sean, his face the color of a blushing stoplight covered in tomatoes and given another coat of red paint just for good measure. "You . . ."

"I . . . uh . . ." Sean gave a weak little smile. "I think you're right. We should probably be leaving now."

"Get out!" the curator shouted.

"Shouldn't we stay and help?" Melissa asked.

He turned to her in disbelief. "You've done enough already. Get out!"

"But—"

"GET OUT!"

"Uh, Misty . . ." Sean took her arm. "I think he wants us to leave."

"GET OUT OF MY MUSEUM!"

Melissa got the point. The two of them scampered up the stairs and dashed for the exit as fast as they could . . . as Mr. Jennings' voice continued echoing down in the basement. "GET OUT! GET OUT OF MY MUSEUM!"

FRIDAY, 17:12 PDST

As they rode their bikes home, Sean knew he and Melissa were thinking exactly the same thing. It wasn't so much what had happened at the museum, but what they had discovered. Was it possible? Could the robber of the jewelry store really have been the knight? Could it really have been the ghost of Sir Richard Falcrest?

Sean had his doubts. But if it wasn't the knight's ghost, then why did it take only the jewels necessary to make the knight's sword?

They rounded the corner, past Mrs. Tubbs' house. She was out front, replanting her petunias. The very petunias they had accidentally destroyed in a race to the radio station less than a week ago.

"Good afternoon, Mrs. Tubbs," Melissa called cheerfully.

But cranky old Mrs. Tubbs didn't answer . . . unless you call grumbling and muttering an answer.

Not that Sean blamed her. No matter how careful

they were, it always seemed the poor lady took the brunt of one of their accidents. (Hmm, maybe she and Mr. Jennings were somehow related.) The accidents were never on purpose (which probably explains why they're called accidents), but it seemed that more often than not, when something went wrong, it included Mrs. Tubbs.

Sean's mind drifted back to the knight . . . and the note it had left behind at the jewelry store. The note that said it needed two other items to complete the sword: gold for the handle and steel for the blade. Did that mean it was going to strike again? If so, where? Where would a knight go for gold . . . and steel? More important—

"Sean, look out!"

Melissa's shout jarred him from his thoughts. He looked up just in time to see the family lawn mower roaring down the street toward him, dragging its stake and rope behind.

Sean veered hard to the right . . . which would have been a good idea, except that's exactly where the mower swerved.

He veered hard to the left. Another good idea, except the mower had just bounced off the curb and was now heading in that direction.

In a final act of desperation, Sean yanked up his handlebars and popped a wheelie.

The front wheel easily missed the mower.

But not the back.

It slammed into the mower, raced up the front end, and sent Sean flying high into the air. It was a beautiful jump, at least a 9.9. Sean couldn't help grinning. As usual, he was pretty impressed with himself. But as usual, the catastrophe wasn't quite over. . . .

Before Sean even hit the ground, he heard Mrs. Tubbs scream. He looked over his shoulder just in time to see the poor lady running for her life. The mower was right behind her and quickly closing the gap. She sprinted toward the house. It would be close, but it looked like she would make it. Unfortunately, you couldn't say the same thing about her flowers . . . because as the mower chased her across the yard, it managed to sheer off every one of her newly planted petunias!

But Sean had little time to worry because moments after he hit the ground he caught a glimpse of his house. Well, it was supposed to be his house. But at the moment it was kind of hard to tell with all of the bubbles pouring out from the windows.

"Look!" Melissa cried.

"I'm looking, I'm looking!"

They arrived at the house and dumped their bikes in the front yard. Bubbles covered everything as a giant mountain of foam slowly oozed its way from the house and down the sidewalk.

Without hesitation, Sean entered the bubbles and began to wade toward the house. But the closer he got to the front door, the taller the mountain of bubbles grew, until it had completely covered his head.

"Sean," Melissa cried from behind, "where are you? I can't see anything but bubbles!"

"Just follow my voice," he shouted as he pushed his way through the suds.

"What happened?" she shouted.

"I don't know!"

"Could it be the dishwasher?" She was right behind him, but he still couldn't see her. "Did you put too much dish soap in the dishwasher?"

"Of course not."

"Are you sure?"

"Sure, I'm sure. Besides, we were out of dish soap."

"What did you use?"

He started to answer, then stopped.

"Sean, what type of soap did you put in?"

Now he knew the problem.

"Sean!"

He also knew she wouldn't let up until he told her.

"Sean!?"

"We were all out of dish soap," he shouted, "so I used your bubble bath."

Melissa's stunned silence said she understood. Good.

That meant he didn't have to tell her the rest . . . especially how he had figured that since it was only bubble bath, he'd go ahead and use a bit more . . . like the entire bottle.

They finally arrived at the door. But he'd no sooner pushed it open when he saw Crash 'n' Burn the hamster dashing out under his feet . . . followed by Clueless, who looked more like a drowned rat than a cat.

And finally Slobs. The poor thing dashed past Sean, nearly knocking him over, as she raced down the walk, howling and baying all the way.

"Catch her!" Melissa cried. "She can't be outside without a leash."

Sean's heart pounded. He knew exactly what she meant. Bloodhounds are incredibly smart, but they can get so caught up in smells and scents that they become blind to everything around them . . . even major dangers.

Sean spun around and began fighting his way back out of the bubbles. "Here, Slobs, come back, girl! Come here, Slobs!"

Melissa joined him, her voice filled with obvious concern. "Slobs, come on, girl!"

Sean continued working his way through the suds when he suddenly heard the squeal of brakes, followed by the dull thud of a body being hit . . . and a single pathetic yelp.

"*Slobs!*" Sean raced through the bubbles until he finally emerged and spotted her. There in the middle of the street, just as he feared, Slobs lay on her side . . . in front of a minivan.

"SLOBS!"

He raced toward her. He could hear Melissa right behind. As they reached the street, the driver, who was already out of the van, was kneeling beside the animal.

Sean arrived, dropping to his knees, his throat tightening with emotion. "Slobs . . . girl. Slobs . . . are you all right?"

But she did not move. He could see her breathing— short, shallow gasps, but other than that her eyes were closed and there was no movement.

"Slobs . . ." Melissa had begun to cry. "Come on, girl, wake up. Slobs . . . come on, girl."

The pain in his sister's voice made Sean's throat grow even tighter.

"Slobs," he urged. "Come on, girl. Come on. . . ."

The driver, an older man, was making some sort of excuse, but Sean didn't hear it. He didn't care. All he could think of was Slobs.

And if she would make it.

4

A Talk With Dad

FRIDAY, 18:45 PDST

"Hey, guys."

Melissa looked up to see Dad enter the waiting room of the animal hospital. Before she knew it, she was on her feet, rushing at him, throwing her arms around him. He held her a long moment, and when she finally looked up, she could see his eyes glistening with moisture.

"I came as soon as I got your message. What did the vet say?" he asked.

"He said . . ." Melissa's voice was husky, and she had to clear it before continuing. "He said she has a severe concussion, a broken leg, and some cracked ribs."

"They're not sure . . ." It was Sean's turn to clear his throat. He sat across the room in one of the chairs. "The doctor said he's not sure if she's going to make it."

Dad nodded but didn't speak. He didn't have to. Melissa knew exactly what he was thinking. These were the same words they'd heard just six months earlier in another reception room . . . in another hospital . . . from another doctor. The words spoken just before Mom had died.

Dad rested his hand on her shoulder and looked at Sean. "Have you guys prayed?"

They both nodded.

More silence. Finally, he spoke. "Listen, why don't you go wait in the car? Let me take care of the paper work here, and I'll be out to join you."

Melissa and Sean nodded, then shuffled across the tiled floor and out the double glass doors toward the van.

FRIDAY, 19:05 PDST

"Well, it's not too bad," Dad said as they stood surveying the soap-bubble damage in the living room.

Melissa and Sean exchanged nervous glances.

"The way I figure, the carpet needed shampooing anyway."

Melissa almost smiled. That's how Dad always dealt with catastrophes—adding just a trace of humor.

"We didn't do it on purpose," Sean explained for the

hundredth time. "We were just trying to get it done a little faster."

"I know," Dad answered.

"You're sure you're not mad?" Melissa asked.

"No . . ." He took a deep breath and slowly let it out. "Actually, I'm getting used to this sort of thing. It's the price one pays for having such bright and creative kids."

This time Melissa did smile.

"So there won't be any punishment?" Sean asked hopefully.

"I don't think so," Dad said as he crossed over to survey the stains on the wall. "Of course you guys will be responsible for repainting these walls."

"Yes, sir," they croaked in unison.

He leaned over to check out the curtains. "And for getting these drapes dry-cleaned."

"Yes, sir."

"And paying for any and all other damages. . . ."

"Yes, sir."

Melissa fidgeted. This was obviously a new definition of the phrase, "no punishment."

But before Dad could come up with any more no-punishment punishments, the phone rang and he crossed to answer it.

Melissa and Sean exchanged relieved glances. For the most part they were off the hook.

"Oh, hello, Mrs. Tubbs." Dad shot a look across the room at them. "Yes, they're right here. . . ."

Then again, maybe not.

SATURDAY, 03:31 PDST

Melissa's heart pounded as she ran through the dense fog. Already her lungs burned, crying out for air. "Slobs," she called. "Where are you, girl? Where are you?"

But there was no answer. Unsure where she was, she slowed, looking for a landmark, for anything to help get her bearings.

But there was nothing. Nothing but thick, impenetrable fog.

Clank.

She caught her breath.

Clank. Clank.

The noise came from straight ahead. Feeling a coldness wrap around her shoulders, she peered through the fog. There was a faint glint of movement . . . a reflection.

Clank! Clank! Clank!

Now she could see it clearly. The knight!

She gasped.

Hearing her, it came to a stop.

She wasn't sure if it saw her or not. Maybe it had only heard her. Then she saw something else.

In its arms. A form. Unmoving.

She leaned forward, straining to see through the fog, careful to make no further sound.

And then she recognized it. An animal. Slobs.

Before she could stop, a scream rose in her throat and burst from her mouth . . . until she suddenly bolted up in bed, wide awake. She sat there, gasping for air, wiping the sweaty hair out of her face when Sean burst into the room.

"What is it?" he cried. "What's the matter?"

Melissa couldn't speak, not yet. She could only sit on her bed, gulping in air as the last of her nightmare slowly faded.

SATURDAY 7: 25 PDST

"Misty, we've had this talk before," Dad said as he scooped up the next round of pancakes from the griddle. Ever since Mom's death, Saturday mornings and pancakes had become a type of tradition for them. A tradition Sean and Melissa might have actually enjoyed . . . if it wasn't for Dad's cooking.

It's not that his pancakes were bad, but when it came to leftovers, even Slobs had turned up her nose at them. Then there was the matter of the garbage disposal. No one was certain, but each Saturday the disposal seemed to be grinding a little more slowly as they shoved the rock-hard remains down into it.

"How can you be so sure?" Sean asked. He was checking out the morning paper while doing his best to gnaw on one of the pancakes. "Why couldn't that knight really be from the past?"

"The Bible is crystal clear," Dad said. "When we die, everyone goes to stand before God. Everyone. Even cruel medieval knights."

"Okay." Melissa nodded. "Then if it's not a ghost or a departed spirit, what is it?"

Dad shook his head. "I don't know. But I do know one thing—you don't have to be afraid of it."

Melissa pushed at her food a long moment. "I don't know, Dad . . . maybe this time we do. . . ."

Sean and Dad both looked at her.

"What if it's, you know . . . what if this knight thing is something else?"

"Such as?"

"You know, from the devil or something."

Sean shifted in his seat.

Dad gently laid down his spatula and pulled up a

chair to join them. "Sweetheart, just because we don't understand something doesn't mean it's from the devil."

"But couldn't this be different? Look at the curse, look at what happened to Slobs, look at—"

"Whoa!" Dad held up his hand. "Hold it a minute. Do you think what happened to Slobs was part of some curse?"

"It could be." Melissa's voice grew slightly unsteady. "Remember what that note said? 'I will unleash my curse upon your city.'"

Dad nodded slowly. "But that curse, it can't apply to you."

"Why not?"

"Because you kids . . . because I pray every day for God's protection over you two, over our entire household."

"Then why did Slobs get hurt?"

Dad held her gaze. "I don't know. I don't always know why bad things happen. I don't know why Slobs got hit. I don't know why your mother . . ." He hesitated a minute, swallowed, then let the phrase trail off. "I can't explain everything. But I can tell you this: God wants us to trust Him. Even when things don't turn out the way we think they should, we know we can trust Him."

Melissa stared hard at the table. Dad reached out and took her hand. "Everyone is afraid at some point, Misty."

She looked up at him. "But you have to remember, He's watching over you. 'If God is for us, who can stand against us?' That's also from the Bible. You've got to trust the Lord, kiddo. Let Him help you fight your battles."

"What if it's something we can't fight?" Melissa asked.

"Like ghosts," Sean chimed in, "or curses . . ."

"Or Slobs?" Melissa asked.

Dad took a long, deep breath and slowly let it out. "Then you pray about it . . . and if necessary, you stand up against it. That's what David did with Goliath. He trusted God and stood up to face what everyone feared."

"That can get pretty scary."

"Of course it can," Dad agreed. "The devil is like a roaring lion—he loves to go around terrifying people. But if you have the faith to stand up to him, the lion becomes all roar and no bite. If you have the faith to stand up and look into its mouth, more often than not you'll see that the lion doesn't even have teeth."

"Teeth?" Melissa looked up with a nervous chuckle. "This one doesn't even have a head."

Dad laughed quietly.

"That might be true," Sean said as he laid the paper out on the table, "but it looks like this one is still doing some roaring."

"What do you mean?" Dad asked.

"Our knight buddy dropped by for another visit last night."

Melissa felt her insides grow a little shaky. "Where?"

Sean read, " 'Hickey's Curiosity and Antique Shoppe.' "

Dad moved in for a better look. "What did it steal this time?"

"Nothing much . . . just some old scabbard."

"Some what?" Melissa asked.

"You know, those long metal cases. . . ." He looked up at her, the truth slowly dawning. "The type they used in the old days to hold their swords."

Melissa caught her breath. Come to think of it, so did Sean and Dad. Each knew exactly what the other was thinking.

Whoever or whatever this knight was, it wasn't finished. It was still preparing its sword. It was still preparing for its "day of vengeance. . . ."

5

Don't Forget Your Vegetables

SATURDAY, 16:50 PDST

When it came to being an older brother, Sean was a pro. He needed Melissa to go with him to stake out the steel mill, and he knew the perfect three-step plan to pull it off:

1. ASK THE EXPECTED QUESTION AND GET THE EXPECTED ANSWER.

"No way," she snapped as she scrubbed and hosed off the bubble stains on the front of the house. "There is no way I'm going to that creepy old steel mill for some stakeout."

2. USE THE RATIONAL APPROACH.

"Look, the knight's already got the rubies and the

scabbard," Sean argued. "It needs only two more things."

"Nope," Melissa said.

"It just needs the gold for the handle and—"

"No way."

"—the steel for the blade."

"Forget it."

"The mill is the only place around here that it could go to forge the steel. It's bound to show up there."

"Absolutely not."

3. AND LAST, BUT MOST IMPORTANT . . . BLACKMAIL.

"All right, if that's the way you want it . . ." Sean hesitated a moment to get her full attention. "I just hope word doesn't get around the neighborhood about all those plantar warts on your feet."

The comment hit its mark. Melissa's mouth dropped open, and the hose went limp in her hand. "I . . . I don't have plantar warts."

"Oh, I know that . . . and you know that . . . but I doubt cute little Bobby Russle or any of the other guys do."

He watched as his sister grew pale.

"You . . . you wouldn't dare," she stammered.

He shrugged. "Who knows . . . but the way I figure it, you don't want to take the chance to find out."

"Sean Robert Hunter . . ." Her voice trembled, but she could find nothing to say.

Sean smiled. Yes, he was good, very good. He turned and started around the house. "Oh," he called over his shoulder. "Make sure to pack some food. It's going to be a long night, and we'll probably get hungry."

He saw the stream of water shooting at him but stepped around the house just in time. Like I said, when it came to being a big brother, Sean was a pro.

SATURDAY 20: 25 PDST

The sun was just setting as they pulled their bikes up to the towering Pierce and Jennings Steel Mill. Sean knew he'd used a dirty trick to get his sister to come, and he almost felt bad about it.

Almost.

But Dad had said it was important that she face her fears, so in reality he was only trying to help. (Then there was the other reality . . . the one where he was scared to death to be here by himself.)

They stashed their bikes in some bushes and found a safe place to hide near the front of the mill. By now everyone had gone home, and there was no telling if or when anybody else would show up. The two had barely settled in before Sean began rummaging through the knapsack. "What did you bring to eat?" he asked. "I'm starved."

"Just the usual stakeout stuff," Misty replied.

Sean continued his search. "Binoculars . . . tape recorder . . . CD player . . . one, two, three, a half-dozen CDs." He gave her a look. "Misty . . ."

"I like being prepared."

He kept digging as his stomach growled in hunger. "Lip gloss, moisturizing cream, shampoo, hair spray, curling iron, toothbrush, toothpaste, dental floss . . ."

"If I die, I gotta look good for the news photo."

"What about food?" Sean demanded as he grew more desperate. "Didn't you bring any—ah, here we go." He reached down and pulled out a giant Tupperware bowl. He opened the lid, then cried, "Broccoli! You brought broccoli? You know I hate broccoli."

He reached for the next container. "Raw cauliflower!" And the next. "Cooked carrots!" He continued opening the others, one after another, faster and faster. "Squash! Asparagus! Turnips! Are you crazy? Where's the real food?"

"Real food?" she asked, blinking innocently.

"You know, the four basic food groups . . . chips, candy, cookies, and cake!?" There was no missing the desperation in his voice. "Come on, sis, where are they?" He pulled out a pitcher. "What's this in here?"

"Carrot juice."

"*Carrot juice?*" His voice squeaked somewhere around a high C. "Are you serious? Everything's vegetables. All you brought is vegetables? You know I hate vegetables!"

Melissa held his look a moment and then quietly answered, "I know, but I hear they're good for curing plantar warts."

Now it was Sean's mouth that dropped open.

Now it was Melissa who was smiling.

And it was just about then that Sean realized she was as good at being a little sister as he was at being a big brother.

Suddenly there was a faint noise.

"Shhh . . ." Melissa whispered.

Sean nodded, hearing it, too. It was around the side of the factory—a scrapping, tapping sound. "It's coming from the fire escape," he whispered. "Somebody's trying to break in by climbing the escape. C'mon."

Before Melissa could protest, Sean left their hiding place, raced to the building, and started moving along the front wall. Not thrilled with being left by herself, she followed.

The mill was built into a hill, with the sides of the building sloping down three stories toward the back. Sean pressed flat against the front wall and continued inching his way toward the corner to sneak a peek.

Melissa followed right behind. "Do you think it could be the—"

"Shhh . . ." He motioned for her to keep quiet.

They arrived at the corner. Then ever so carefully, Sean eased his head around it to take a look. Once he was sure the coast was clear, he scooted around the corner and motioned for Melissa to follow.

The noise up on the fire escape grew louder.

"Sean?" she asked nervously.

"Shhh!"

"I just want to make sure you see those—"

"Will you be quiet?" he whispered. "Real professionals know when to talk and when to keep quiet."

"I just don't want you falling over those—"

He turned and glared at her. "And right now a real professional would . . . AHHHH!"

CLANG, BANG, RATTLE, RATTLE

The AHHHH! was Sean shouting as he fell.

The *clang, bang, rattle, rattle* were the garbage cans that he'd just fallen into. The poor guy flipped and flopped this way and that, trying to get to his feet. He finally spotted Melissa and reached out to her for help.

A good idea, except for the part where he pulled too

hard and threw her off balance, dragging her directly on top of him and on even more of those lovely garbage cans.

CLANG, BANG, RATTLE, RATTLE
CLANG, BANG, RATTLE, RATTLE.

Now they were making twice the noise, but with one extra little surprise. The force of Melissa's fall was just strong enough to send all of them—cans, brother, and sister—rolling and bouncing down the steep hill.

"WHOA . . ."

Clang, bang, rattle.

"WHAA . . ."

Rattle, bang, clang.

"EEEE . . ."

Roll, rattle, roll, rattle, roll.

Everything was a blur of arms, legs, and cans. Garbage flew in all directions. And by the time they'd reached the bottom of the hill, it was hard to tell where the kid left off and the slimy, stinky, dripping garbage began.

But the fun and games weren't over yet. Not quite.

It seems there was a little dropoff at the bottom of the

hill. A little dropoff that ended directly above one of those not-so-little trash dumpsters on wheels.

The good news was their style and form were incredible. In fact, as they dove off the hill and tumbled head over heels through the air, Sean was even thinking of trying out for the US Olympic Diving Team.

But Melissa's thoughts ran a little differently. "WE'RE GONNA DIE!"

Of course they didn't. That would have been too easy. Instead, they landed inside the giant dumpster with a tremendous

CRASH!

followed by the gentle

pitter, patter, splatter

of garbage raining down upon them.

And still the catastrophe continued. . . .

The force of impact caused the whole dumpster to start rolling down the rest of the hill.

"Wh-wh-wh-wh-what's hap-p-p-pen-ing-ing-ing?" Melissa cried from inside the bouncing dumpster.

With the slimy bottom and all that bouncing, it took most of Sean's effort just to struggle to his feet. But at last he was able to take a peek over the top.

He wished he hadn't.

"Wh-wh-wh-where are-re-re-re we-e-e-e going-ing-ing?" Melissa cried.

"Nowh-wh-wh-where!" he shouted.

"Wh-wh-wh-at?"

"There's a tre-e-e, dead-d-d-d ahead-d-d-d!"

"Wh-wh-wh-at?"

"I said there's a tree-e-e-e, dead-d-d-d—"

BANG!

The dumpster finally come to a stop.
Unfortunately, so had Sean's consciousness.
The guy was out cold.

SATURDAY 20: 35 PDST

When Sean came to, he saw Melissa staring down at him. Well, at least he thought it was Melissa. It was kinda hard to tell with all the garbage hanging from her.

"Sean . . . Sean, can you hear me? Sean?"

"Yeah," he groaned. "I hear you fine." He struggled to sit up. By the looks of things, they'd been thrown out of the dumpster when they'd hit the tree. And by his throbbing head, he knew exactly what he'd landed on. He winced and reached up to touch his aching temples. Unfortunately, he touched a hanging banana peel instead. Angrily, he yanked it off and flung it aside.

He looked over at the mill. The fire escape hovered above them in the evening shadows. "Did you see it?" he asked Melissa. "Did it get away?"

"Uh, not exactly."

"Then where is it?" Sean asked as he peered into the darkness. "I don't see it."

"Oh, it's still there."

"Where?"

"On the fire escape."

His eyes shot up and down the stairs. "There's no one there."

"Look up a little higher, at the very top."

Sean strained to see through the darkness. "I don't see—" And then he saw it. He blinked, hoping it wasn't true, that maybe he was seeing things because of his fall. But of course he wasn't.

"A raccoon?" he groaned.

"Looks like it," Melissa said.

"We went through all of this over a raccoon?"

"Right again."

Sean groaned and lay back down. Unfortunately, it was directly into a pile of somebody's half-eaten salad, complete with lettuce, cucumbers, radishes, shredded carrots, and some very smashed tomatoes. He did not move, but continued lying there, staring up in the air. And then ever so quietly, he muttered, "I really, really hate vegetables. . . ."

6

The Meeting

It had been a half hour since their little ride in the trash bin. Other than Sean's bruised head (not to mention his bruised ego), everything was pretty much back to normal . . . except for the distinct odor of garbage that seemed to follow them wherever they went.

By now it was dark, and as they rode through town, Melissa was anxious to get home. She was glad for the overhead streetlights, but she figured there were still a few too many dark shadows lurking around just a few too many dark corners.

"You sure this is the quickest way home?" she asked.

"Sure, I'm sure," Sean said. "You're still not chicken, are you?"

She hated it when he read her mind like that. "No, of

course not," she lied. But she could tell by the smirk on his face that he knew better.

"Wait a minute." He suddenly slowed his bike. "What's that?"

"Come on, Sean, I'm not falling for that old one."

"No, I'm serious."

Melissa rolled her eyes. She knew her brother loved her and if the chips were down he would do anything for her. But she also knew he would do anything for a good joke. And this was one joke she was definitely not about to fall—

Clank.

Then again, maybe she would.

Clank. Clank.

They brought their bikes to a screeching stop.

"What is it?" she whispered.

"Sounds like metal."

Clank.

He motioned to the nearby alley. "It's coming from in there."

Melissa sighed. Since their adventure at the steel mill, she'd been looking forward to getting home and taking a nice, hot shower . . . with plenty of soap. But it looked like her brother had other ideas. "I suppose as 'professionals,' you think we're supposed to go in there and check that noise out?" she asked.

He nodded. "We're a detective agency, Misty. This is what detective agencies do."

Clank! Clank! Clank!

"C'mon."

He hopped off his bicycle and walked it toward the front of Bowman's Coin Shop. Reluctantly, Melissa followed. They leaned their bikes against the building and silently crossed around the side to the alley.

It was dark. A single streetlamp lit the entire area. It cast all sorts of strange and creepy shadows. Luckily, none of those creepy shadows were moving.

"Maybe . . . maybe it was just the wind," Melissa whispered.

Clank.

They froze.
"Then again, maybe not."

Clank. Clank.

"That's definitely metal," Sean whispered.
"Maybe it could be another raccoon or something."

Clank! Clank! Clank!

"Only if it's wearing a suit of armor," Sean answered.

Suddenly the noise stopped. Now there was nothing but silence.

"What happened?" Melissa whispered. "Where did it go?"

"I can't tell. I can't see a thing from here. I'm going to cross the alley and duck behind that old pickup."

"Are you crazy?" Melissa whispered. "If you step into the open, it'll see you for sure."

"Do you have any better ideas?"

"Going home?" Melissa asked hopefully.

"C'mon. Once we get across, we'll be able to see everything."

"What do you mean, 'we'?"

"You want to stay here by yourself?"

It was an old ploy, but it worked every time. "All right," she muttered, "but if we die, you're going to live to regret it."

"C'mon."

Sean took off. Melissa followed. A second later they were on the other side of the alley behind the pickup. Melissa's heart pounded like a jackhammer. Slowly, ever so slowly, they lifted their heads above the hood of the truck to take a peek.

And there, coming out of the back of the coin shop, was a walking suit of armor. The reflection from the streetlight gave it an unearthly glow.

"It's the knight," Melissa gasped.

As if hearing her, the knight stopped and slowly turned in their direction.

"Don't move," Sean whispered. "Don't move a muscle."

Clank.

It started toward them.

Clank. Clank.

Melissa's heart went into double time.

"No way can it see us," Sean whispered. "There're too many shadows, and we're too well hidden."

Clank! Clank! Clank!

"Maybe you should tell *it* that," Melissa said as the knight continued its approach.

"Shhh . . ." he whispered. "It can't possibly see us. It's got to pass by. Just lay low."

And still the thing came toward them.

Clank. Clank.

Instinctively, the two dropped lower behind the truck.

By now Melissa's heart was pounding so hard she thought it would explode inside her chest. Any second it would be there. Any second it would round the truck and loom above them and—

Clank! Clank! Clank!

Wait a minute! Was it her imagination, or was the clanking starting to fade? Yes, it was moving past them, moving past the truck and heading out the alley.

Melissa took a long, deep breath and let it out. Then, to her horror, she saw Sean rising to his feet to get a better look.

"What are you doing?" she whispered. "Get back down."

He shook his head and motioned for her to join him. At first she refused, but as the sound continued to fade, she slowly rose.

That's when the knight came to a stop.

Melissa went ice cold.

Slowly, its head swiveled to face them. Neither Melissa nor Sean moved. It was too late. They'd been spotted. They'd been spotted, and there was nothing they could do about it.

But instead of coming after them, it remained standing there at the opening of the alley. Its shiny metal glowed and shimmered under the streetlamp.

Melissa wanted to run, to make a break for it, but she didn't trust herself. It's hard running on legs of Jell-O. Besides, there was one other minor problem.

The alley behind Bowman's Coin Shop was a dead end. There was only one way out . . . and the knight stood directly in the middle of that way.

Melissa grew colder. She found it more difficult to breathe. What would happen next? What would it do?

Unfortunately, she didn't have to wait long.

Ever so slowly the knight raised its great steel arm until it pointed directly at them.

"*You!*" it shouted.

If Melissa thought she was shaking before, she was now registering a 9.5 on the Richter Scale.

With its other hand, the knight reached for the helmet's visor.

Now it would happen. Now they would finally see him. They would look directly into its face, into those long-dead eyes, and—

The visor gave an ominous creak as the knight shoved it up to reveal . . .

Nothing.

There were no eyes, there was no face. There wasn't even a head. Nothing but a black, terrifying void.

Melissa and Sean gasped.

Once again the thundering voice boomed from the

armor. "You of the Hunter clan!"

Neither Melissa or Sean Hunter particularly felt like answering. Besides, it's hard answering when your heart is in your throat.

The voice continued. "Follow me not, for your time comes soon enough!"

Then without another word, the knight closed its face visor, turned, and lumbered out of the alley and out of sight.

7

More Clues

Immediately after church let out, Melissa was running down the street toward the animal hospital. Her encounter with Sir Richard Falcrest the night before hadn't done much to ease her fears about Slobs.

Nor had the headline in this morning's paper:

"Gold Coins Missing in Robbery"

Things were coming true exactly as the knight had threatened. First the rubies to decorate the sword, then the scabbard, and now the gold coins, which it was obviously going to melt down to make the sword's handle.

And if all these were coming true, then what about its

other threat? The one involving the curse on the townspeople?

And finally, to top it all off, there was the minor fact that the knight actually knew them by name:

> *"You of the* Hunter *clan! Follow me not,*
> *for your time comes soon enough."*

Yes, sir, if ever there was a time to be majorly worried, Melissa figured it was now. She raced up the steps to the animal hospital, threw open the doors, and ran into the lobby.

The receptionist looked up, somewhat startled. "May I help you?"

"Yes," Melissa answered, trying to catch her breath. "Our dog . . . Slobbers . . . I just came to . . . that is, I wonder if I could—"

"Hello, Misty." Dr. Troast had just appeared around the corner.

"Hello, Doctor." She took in another gulp of air. "I know you said you would call if there was any change in Slobs, but . . . I mean a lot of stuff's been happening and—"

"You wanted to see how she is doing?" he asked. Melissa nodded.

"Well, right now she is sleeping soundly. It's important she get her rest. When she wakes, I'll examine her again and give you a call."

Melissa's heart sank. She tried again. "I appreciate that, but can I . . . I mean would it be possible for me to take just a little peek at her?"

Dr. Troast looked at her. She held his gaze, hoping he could see her urgency. Finally, he broke into a little smile. "All right . . . but just for a moment. And you must be careful not to wake her."

Melissa nodded eagerly.

He motioned for her to follow. She rounded the counter to join him, and they headed down the hallway, entering a large room to the left. It was full of all sorts of cats and dogs in cages. Melissa slowed to a stop as she searched for Slobs. Her eyes scanned row after row, but the dog was nowhere to be found. A quiet panic rose up inside as she searched again. Maybe Slobs had been too injured. Maybe the doctor didn't have the heart to tell her. Maybe Slobs was already—

No. Melissa pushed the thought out of her mind. She wouldn't, she *couldn't* think that.

"Misty?"

She looked over to see Dr. Troast standing in a doorway at the other end of the room. "She's in here."

With a wave of relief, Melissa followed the doctor into the other room. It was much smaller. There were only three cages. Two were empty. The last one held Slobs.

Melissa sucked in her breath. Slobs was there all right, but she lay completely unmoving, and she looked so small and helpless. Her right back leg was bandaged. A tube was taped to her left foreleg and ran up to a plastic bottle suspended on a stand next to the cage. Large leather straps were buckled across her body.

"She . . ." Melissa swallowed back the knot growing in her throat. "She doesn't . . . look so good."

"She's been through quite a lot," the doctor answered.

Melissa nodded and looked on, feeling the knot grow.

"Don't worry about that tube," he said. "It's putting medicine into her. And the straps are to hold her still so she won't pull it out."

Melissa nodded but could already feel her eyes starting to burn with moisture. Slobs had been one of the last gifts their mother had given her and her brother. And if anything were ever to happen to her . . .

She felt Dr. Troast's hand rest on her shoulder. "Right now all we can do is let her sleep," he whispered.

Melissa nodded and swiped at her eyes. "How about praying?" she asked.

The doctor smiled. "Praying is always a good idea."

SUNDAY, 11:52 PDST

Running into Sir Richard Falcrest the night before and reading the morning's headlines hadn't done much for Sean's nerves, either. But unlike his sister, when Sean got scared, he got mad. Which explains why, instead of visiting Slobs, he'd headed back to the Middleton Museum to do a little more investigating. He wasn't sure what he'd find, but anything was better than sitting around waiting to be attacked by some invisible knight or curse or whatever.

As he entered the museum, he was glad to see that Mr. Jennings, the curator, was nowhere in sight. He headed over to the stairs and quickly made his way down into the Medieval Room. He was also glad that Mclissa had stayed behind. It could really be a nuisance keeping your little sister calm and relaxed . . . while having to make up excuses as to why your own knees were knocking so loudly.

By now all the suits of armor were pieced together and back in place. Sean moved past them until he finally arrived at Sir Richard Falcrest's display. As before, it stood by itself on a platform, towering above him as silent and menacing as ever.

Sean could no longer hear his knees knocking together. It was hard to hear anything over the chattering of his teeth. It's not that he was afraid, it's just that dying on a Sunday afternoon can really be a drag . . . especially when you're on summer break and there's no school the next day.

He remembered what Dad had said about facing up to his fears, about looking into the lion's mouth. He wasn't particularly fond of the idea but knew it had to be done. After a deep breath, he stepped up to the display, crossed his arms, and glared up at the figure. . . . The helmet. The chest piece, half covered by the shield held across it. The leggings of steel. And finally the boots.

It was then he noticed something he hadn't seen before . . . a dirty smudge on the left boot.

Can ghosts get dirty? he wondered.

He glanced at the plaque that Melissa had started to read earlier. He took a step closer and started reading it himself. It seemed long (let's face it, reading anything longer than a bubble gum wrapper seemed long to Sean), but the last part caught his attention. It dealt with the villagers from where Sir Richard Falcrest had lived.

> *Be it known the village stablemen—*
> *Tom Morrisey, Peter Hickey, and the tailor,*
> *John Bowman—all raised arms against the*
> *great Lord Falcrest.*

Sean stopped reading. Weren't those the same last

names as the recent robbery victims'? *Morrisey* Jewelers, *Hickey's* Antiques, and *Bowman's* Coin Shop? Was it possible? Were all the people being robbed actually descendants of those who overthrew Sir Richard Falcrest? Sean swallowed hard. He wasn't crazy about this idea, not one bit. He continued reading.

> *Though this be true, the greatest blame*
> *falleth upon two men who first hatched*
> *the plot: the town miller, Deacon Pierce. . . .*

Again Sean stopped. Pierce, Pierce . . . where had he heard the name Pierce? Morrisey for the rubies, Hickey for the scabbard, Bowman for the gold handle . . . and Pierce for the—suddenly he got it. Of course. The *Pierce* and Jennings Steel Mill! That's where the knight would go to get the steel for its blade. It was just as Sean had suspected. It *had* to be the scene of the next robbery.

But he still wasn't finished with the plaque. There was one last sentence to read.

> *Although Pierce was the ringleader, let it be*
> *known that his partner in the plot was the*
> *village blacksmith, Jacob Hunter.*

Again Sean tried to swallow, but this time there was nothing left in his mouth to swallow.

"Jacob *Hunter*." Could this be one of his own ancestors? Could he and Melissa be descendants of this very villager . . . the one whom the knight hated and blamed the most?

His mind whirled. No wonder the knight knew their names . . . they were also on his list of vengeance! What had he said the night before?

> *"You of the* Hunter *clan! Follow me not,*
> *for your time comes soon enough!"*

Fear gripped Sean. For the briefest second he wanted to turn, he wanted to run. But remembering what Dad had said, he forced himself to stay. He forced himself to continue looking into the mouth of the lion. He could feel his body trembling, and he knew his heart was pounding a mile a minute. But after whispering a little prayer, he forced himself to remain.

And it was then that he noticed something else.

The bottom half of the plaque seemed to be different from the top half. It was hard to tell in the dim light, but the part mentioning all of their names looked different . . . newer. As if it had been written later.

Suspicion began to replace the fear. Something was up. Could somebody have added the bottom half to that plaque? Could somebody have added on those names? But why would anybody want to do that? Why would anybody add the names of all those people being robbed . . . unless . . . Sean frowned. Unless that person was somehow justifying the robberies. . . .

But who? Sean stared at the plaque. He really couldn't be certain. Maybe it was all the same plaque. Maybe his eyes were just playing tricks on him. There had to be some way to make sure. Some way to see if the bottom half of the plaque was as old as the top half . . .

Suddenly an idea came to mind.

He spun around and raced for the stairs. Unfortunately, he ran smack dab into someone carrying an armload of files. Well, whoever it was *had* been carrying an armload of files. Now those files were busy flying into the air and fluttering to the ground.

"I'm sorry!" Sean exclaimed. "Are you all right?"

The man turned around, and Sean saw he was face-to-face with none other than . . . the curator, Mr. Jennings.

"Oh no . . ." Sean groaned.

"You're that Hunter boy!" Jennings stammered.

"Yes, sir," Sean answered. "I'm sorry. I really am sorry."

Jennings snorted in frustration and bent over to start picking up the papers.

Sean dropped to his knees and joined him. "Here, let me—"

"No, just go on. You've done enough already!"

But Sean knew he should stay to help, so he did. Well . . . at least for another 7.3 seconds.

That was the amount of time it took before they both reached for the same piece of paper. That was the amount of time it took before Sean accidentally knocked into Mr. Jennings . . . throwing him off balance, sending him staggering, until he stumbled into—you guessed it— one of the suits of armor . . . which fell into another suit of armor, which fell into another . . . and on and on it went, just like old times.

The two watched in numb astonishment. When Sean finally turned to Mr. Jennings, he could see the man's face was once again turning bright red. His mouth was already open, and he was already sputtering, trying to find the words.

Sean figured he'd save him the trouble. "I know," he said, turning and starting for the stairs. "I'm going, I'm going. . . ."

SUNDAY, 15:56 PDST

Three and a half hours had passed since Sean had played his second game of dominoes with the armor. Now he and Melissa were once again riding their bikes. Only this time it was toward Doc's house.

"Are you sure that plaque had everyone's name on it?" Melissa asked.

Sean nodded. "Everyone that the knight has robbed."

"Along with ours?"

Again Sean nodded. "Along with ours."

"So that proves the curse is true," Melissa said. "It proves that the knight came after them, that it somehow hurt Slobs, and—" she gulped—"it proves that it'll be coming after us."

"Maybe . . . but that doesn't explain the bottom part of the plaque."

"What about it?"

"When I got close to it, I could see that the bottom part—the part with the names on it—looked newer."

Before Melissa could quiz him any further, they arrived at Doc's house and were interrupted by a pathetic, high-pitched roar that sounded like a lawn mower caught in a blender. They turned and watched as Doc slowly appeared, floating above the roof.

"What is she up to?" Sean cried over the noise. "How's she doing that?"

"Look at her tennis shoes!" Melissa shouted. "They've got little helicopter blades on them!"

"Hi, guys!"

Melissa and Sean both gave a jump as Jeremiah appeared on Melissa's wristwatch. "Pretty cruel, huh?"

"Cruel?" Sean shouted.

"I think he means, 'cool,' " Melissa corrected as they got off their bikes. "It's pretty *cool*."

Jeremiah nodded. "You took the words left out of my mouth."

Melissa sighed, but before she could correct him, Sean shouted, "What about the Age Detector? I thought she was working on the Age Detector."

"Oh, that's yesterday's news. Now we've got bigger fish to fly."

The three looked back up at Doc. It was a beautiful sight . . . except for the part where the woman's legs weren't strong enough to keep her upright and the little propellers raised her feet higher and higher . . . while her body sank lower and lower. In a matter of seconds poor Doc was suddenly doing some very impressive midair splits.

"Boy," Sean cried, "I bet that hurts."

But she wasn't done yet. Ever so slowly, her body started to tumble forward. The good news was she was no longer doing the splits. The bad news was she was beginning to tumble. With both legs spread apart, she began going around and around. . . .

"Shouldn't we do something?" Melissa shouted.

"Not much we can do," Jeremiah called, "at least until she runs out of gas."

"What about the off switch!" Sean yelled.

"A great idea!" Jeremiah called. "When she comes down, I'll remind her to add one."

Melissa and Sean glanced at each other and shook their heads.

"Listen," Sean shouted, "do you suppose we could borrow that Age Detector thingie? We gotta check out the age of something."

"We do?" Melissa asked.

"That's why we came here. We're going to borrow the Age Detector to see how old that plaque is at the museum."

"Oh," Melissa nodded, grateful to finally be clued in on his plan. But she wasn't particularly grateful that the plan involved heading back to face the suit of armor.

"You don't mind if we borrow it?" Sean repeated to Jeremiah.

"Be my pest," the little guy chirped. "Go upstairs and hinder yourselves."

Sean looked at Melissa.

"He means 'help' ourselves," she explained.

Sean nodded and called, "Thanks!"

As they headed up the porch, Melissa asked, "How long before Doc runs out of gas?"

"Just another three hours, twenty-two minutes, and seventeen seconds," Jeremiah answered.

Melissa closed her eyes and shook her head. Poor Doc. Then again, she wondered which fate was worse . . . not being able to land for a few more hours . . . or heading back to the museum and becoming dead forever.

8

Trapped

"But why can't we see the Falcrest exhibit?" Sean asked.

The clerk at the museum's information desk pushed up her glasses and patiently explained, "We had a little accident downstairs in the Medieval Room. It is closed for repairs."

"Accident?" Melissa asked.

The clerk nodded. "Apparently, someone knocked over the entire display of armored knights."

"No kidding," Sean said with wide-eyed innocence. "Now, who would do something like that?"

The receptionist shook her head. "It was quite a messy affair. I'm afraid it won't be open for at least another day."

"Another day?" Sean exclaimed. He adjusted the heavy knapsack on his shoulders . . . the one containing the Age Detector. "We can't wait that long."

The clerk tried to crank up a smile. "I know that exhibit has become quite the attraction, with all of the robberies around town. But surely you can wait one or two more days."

Melissa and Sean exchanged glances.

"Do you think . . ." Melissa cleared her throat. "Couldn't we take just one little peek?"

The woman shook her head. "I'm sorry. The museum is about to close and—"

"It would only take a minute."

"As I have previously stated, the exhibit is currently—"

"We understand," Sean quickly interrupted. He grabbed Melissa's arm and started pulling her away. "We'll try again tomorrow."

"What?" Melissa asked in surprise.

"Come along," he said.

"What are you doing?" she protested as he moved her away. "It will only take a—"

"Come along!" he repeated.

Melissa was about to start another one of their award-winning arguments, when she suddenly saw the reason behind Sean's urgency. Mr. Jennings was approaching. They quickly moved away from the main lobby and headed into the Native American exhibit. "Is he still there?" Sean asked.

Melissa looked over her shoulder. "Yeah."

"Is he following us?"

"I can't tell."

"Keep walking."

"Sean, this is stupid."

"Keep walking."

"It's been three days since your little catastrophe. Surely he's forgiven you by now."

"I wouldn't bet on it."

"It was a freak accident, a once-in-a-lifetime thing."

"Uh, actually, more like *twice* in a lifetime."

She turned to him.

"Remember, I said I was here earlier today?"

A look of realization slowly filled her face. "No," she said. "You didn't . . ."

He gave a painful nod. "Just keep walking."

They crossed through the Indian exhibit, then the Mexico exhibit, then a half-dozen more displays before they finally entered the Prehistoric Room. In the center of this exhibit was the museum's pride and joy . . . a life-sized replica of a brontosaurus. And not just some fake skeleton, we're talking the whole ball of wax—fake skin, fake muscle, fake everything—so realistic that it almost looked alive.

"What are we going to do?" Melissa asked. "How can we check out the age of that plaque if we can't even get down to the basement to see it?"

"Relax," Sean whispered. He glanced up to the dinosaur towering above them.

"But—"

"Trust me." He grinned. "I've got a plan."

Melissa took a deep breath and slowly let it out. "That's exactly what I'm afraid of."

SUNDAY, 17:25 PDST

"Is it safe?" Melissa whispered.

"Yeah," Sean called, "everyone's gone."

"You sure?"

"Yeah, you can come out now. Just grab the rope and start climbing."

It had been nearly a half hour since Sean had thought of climbing up into the brontosaurus's mouth to hide. All it took was borrowing the ladder being used to repair a hanging pterodactyl, and then plenty of squirming and wiggling as they squished themselves into the mouth together.

At first Melissa had protested, "This is crazy."

But Sean had insisted it was perfect. "We hide in the dinosaur's mouth, wait until the museum closes, then we climb out and go down into the basement to check out the plaque with the Age Detector. No sweat."

And for the most part, he had been right. Getting inside the mouth really hadn't been a problem. It was getting back out that got tricky. It might have been less tricky if Melissa had managed to stay there. But since they were both crammed inside . . . and since she was the one farthest back toward the throat . . . and since the throat was made of slick fiberglass . . . well, it wasn't too long before Sean squirmed one too many times, forcing her to lose her balance, causing her to slip and slide all the way down the throat

"WOAHHHhhh . . ."

Until she landed in its belly.

Thunk.

She wasn't hurt, but she wasn't thrilled, either. "I thought these things were vegetarians," she called from inside the creature. "They're not supposed to eat people."

"Stay there while I go get a rope," Sean had ordered.

Having no other place to go, Melissa figured she'd obey.

A few minutes later Sean had found a rope and had thrown it down to her.

"Just grab it and pull yourself up."

It wasn't easy, but with lots of effort, Melissa managed to climb back up the throat and into the mouth. From there she was able to step outside and onto the ladder. It was great to finally see daylight again. Well, what little daylight there was. Apparently, when they'd closed the museum, they'd also shut off the lights. All of them.

"Great," she sighed as she moved down the ladder. "Do you have any idea how to get to the basement from here in the dark?"

"No problem," Sean answered. "Trust me."

She groaned. "I thought we already tried that."

Unfortunately, she was right. Within twenty minutes Sean had gotten them so lost that Melissa thought they'd never get out. Then there was the matter of the shadows. The ones that seemed to lurk and loom wherever she looked.

"It's just around this next corner," Sean called over his shoulder. "I'm sure of it."

Melissa sighed and followed his voice. "That's what you said about the last seven corners. I don't want to complain, but if you ask me—"

Suddenly a huge arm reached out and grabbed her!

She let out a scream and began fighting the giant, hairy creature. But try as she might, she could not break free of its grip. She hit and kicked and clawed, but nothing worked.

Then she tried something new. She tripped and fell. But the creature fell right along with her, its arms still locked around her in a deadly embrace.

"Misty!" Sean called. "Misty!"

After plenty more kicks, hits, and a few screams thrown in for good measure, Melissa finally managed to break free of the thing. Desperate to get away, she started crawling on her hands and knees.

"Misty!"

She staggered to her feet and ran directly into a large clump of trees. Trees filled with lots of long, slithering things. Long, slithering things that looked and felt exactly like—

"SNAKES!" she screamed.

She grabbed them off her arms and flug them away. But others continued falling. For every one she peeled off, three more fell in its place. "GET THEM OFF!" she screamed. "GET THEM OFF! GET THEM OFF!"

"Hang on!" Sean shouted. "Don't panic!"

But panicking seemed like a pretty good idea as the snakes continued raining down upon her arms, her shoulders, her hair. "GET THEM OFF! GET THEM OFF! GET THEM OFF!"

Melissa stumbled out of the exhibit, slapping at them and yanking them off, when she suddenly ran face-to-face with something even more hideous . . . and terrifying . . . grotesquely human yet not human at all. Menacing lips curled into a sneer, crazed eyes glared at her. Melissa tried to scream, but she couldn't find her voice. Come to think of it, she couldn't find her breath, either. And then, just when the room started to spin, just when her head was growing light and she was about to pass out . . .

Sean managed to find the lights. Suddenly the room was bathed in brightness. Blinding, wonderful, beautiful brightness.

"Are you okay?" he called in concern.

Melissa managed to nod as she leaned over, trying to catch her breath. She looked about the room. They were standing in the African exhibit. Across the floor, lying on its side, was her first attacker. A stuffed gorilla. She turned toward the stand of trees. Like the gorilla, they were also fake . . . as were the dozens of rubber snakes lying on the floor. Finally, she turned to the hideous face beside her. It was a tribal war mask made of fiberglass.

"None of it's real," she gasped, still trying to catch her breath. "It's all . . . fake."

Sean nodded. "Yeah."

She threw him a look, expecting some sort of wisecrack. But he said nothing. Instead, he approached her and actually looked concerned. "You sure you're okay?"

Again she nodded, only this time she fought off an involuntary shudder. And then another. She was starting to shiver. Immediately, Sean's jacket was off and he was wrapping it around her shoulders.

"Thanks," she whispered.

He nodded, then glanced around the room. "It's just like Dad said, isn't it? Sometimes the very things we're afraid of . . . when we stop and look at them, we see that they're fake, that they really don't have any teeth at all."

Melissa nodded and looked at the floor surrounding her . . . the gorilla, the snakes, the mask. It was true, everything she'd been afraid of, everything she'd freaked over, was a fake.

Clank.

They froze and listened.

Clank. Clank.

It was coming closer.

Melissa turned to Sean. "Do you think . . ." Her voice caught, and she tried again. "Do you think it's just a guard?"

Clank. Clank. Clank.

"Not unless he's wearing metal boots."

Instinctively, Melissa backed up, moving toward the nearest wall. Sean headed back to the switch.

Clank. Clank. Clank. Clank.

She saw him reach for the lights, and a moment later they were standing in total darkness. . . .

9

Facing the Lion

Sean held his breath as the sound of the knight's footsteps approached.

Clank. Clank.

He pressed flatter against the wall, trying his best to blend into the shadows, yet wondering if it would do any good—wondering if ghosts could see in the dark.

Clank. Clank. Clank.

He began to pray. Nothing long or detailed. He wasn't interested in *how* God would save them, just that he *would* save them. He hadn't even finished before—

Clank. Clank.

Was it possible? The noise seemed to be changing direction.

Clank. Clank. Clank.

Yes, the footsteps were fading away. Sean breathed a quiet prayer of thanks, then whispered over to Melissa, "It's moving away."

"Yeah," she agreed.

"Great, let's follow it."

"Are you crazy!?" she demanded.

"It'll know the way out. C'mon." Sean moved from the wall and started out of the room.

"Sean . . ." Melissa whispered after him. "Sean!"

After a few minutes he heard her start to follow. They moved from one exhibit to another. He could still hear the *clank*ing, but it was off in the distance. He planned to keep it that way—just stay close enough to follow the sound, but no closer.

Four, maybe five, minutes passed until they finally saw glimpses of the late afternoon sun pouring through the lobby windows. Sean eased around the last corner just in time to see the knight open one of the front doors and disappear outside.

"What's going on?" Melissa whispered from behind.

"It's gone."

She breathed a sigh of relief. It sounded like such a

good idea that Sean tried it, too.

"Now what?" she asked.

"Well, Plan One would be to follow him. Or Plan Two—"

"I vote for Plan Two," she interrupted.

Sean saw her point. He wasn't thrilled about taking the chance of running into the knight again, either.

"By the way," Melissa asked, "what is Plan Two?"

"I'm not sure. Probably going back down into the basement and checking out the age of that plaque."

"And I had to ask," she muttered.

They made their way across the lobby and over to the basement stairs. As they headed down the steps, it grew darker and darker. This time, however, Sean found the light switch early. They winced as the fluorescents flickered on.

There, in front of them, were the dozens of suits of armor all sprawled out across the floor.

"Nice work," Melissa said.

Sean nodded. "Practice makes perfect."

They both looked over to the stand holding Sir Richard Falcrest. It was completely untouched. Well, untouched except for it being completely empty. The armor was nowhere to be seen. Without a word, they crossed toward it. When they arrived, Melissa stooped down to examine the plaque.

"See where it looks like another part's been added?" Sean asked. "Down at the bottom where the names are."

Melissa looked closer and nodded. She rose and stepped back. "Go ahead and fire up that Age Detector thingie," she said. "Let's see what it says."

Sean set down his backpack and quickly pulled out the cone-shaped machine. He found the power switch and snapped it on.

It hummed loudly.

"Wait a minute," Melissa said. "The paste . . . we need to put the paste on the cone."

Sean nodded as Melissa reached into the pack and pulled out the jar of thick, brown gunk. She unscrewed the lid and made a face as she dipped her hand into the goo. But this was no time to be squeamish. She pulled out a giant blob and quickly spread it over the cone.

"That's good," Sean said. "Now stand back."

She didn't have to be told twice.

"Here goes nothing!"

They both braced themselves as Sean aimed the cone at the plaque and pulled the trigger.

But this time there was no smoke, no explosion, and no deafening *Boing-ing-ings.*

There was only a louder hum.

Sean glanced down at the digital readout on top of

the cone. "It reads, four years, eleven months, and twelve days," he said.

"That makes sense," Melissa said as she stepped a little closer. "That's about how long this exhibit's been here. Now aim it down at that bottom half of the plaque."

Sean readjusted the cone and pointed it toward the bottom of the plaque. A brand-new set of figures appeared. "Two days, twelve hours, and sixteen minutes," he said.

Melissa caught her breath. "That means somebody's just added it!"

Sean nodded. "So the curse *isn't* for real. There's no ghost, just someone who added all these names. But why?"

Melissa moved in and reread the names: "*Morrisey* . . . as in Morrisey Jewelers. *Hickey* . . . as in Hickey's Antiques. And *Bowman* . . . as in Bowman's Coin Shop. They're all there. Exactly in the order they were robbed."

"Except for this last one," Sean said. He pointed to the name and read, "Deacon *Pierce*."

Melissa looked at him.

"*Pierce* . . ." he repeated. "As in *Pierce* and Jennings Steel Mill."

"You think that's where he's going next?"

Sean nodded. "I know he is. And I bet he's going

there right now. Whoever our wannabe ghost is, you can bet he's on his way to finally forge his sword at the steel mill."

Melissa swallowed. "So what do we do?"

Sean looked at her. He didn't like giving the answer any more than she liked hearing it. "I think we need to go there and expose him."

"You mean look into the lion's mouth?" Melissa asked.

Sean slowly nodded. "I'm afraid so."

SUNDAY, 18:50 PDST

Twenty minutes later the two were on their bikes, approaching the Pierce and Jennings Steel Mill. The sun hung low in the sky, and when they arrived the Mill was deserted . . . except for a single pickup, whose driver's-side door was still open.

"What's that doing here?" Melissa asked.

Sean squinted at the building. "Looks like our knight couldn't find a horse."

"What do you mean?"

He pointed. "Over there by the building."

Melissa looked and fought back a cold shiver. There it was . . . the knight. Fifty yards away. It was striding away from the building and holding a large can of gasoline, which it was pouring out onto the ground.

Suddenly a voice called from her digital watch, "Hey, guys, what's baking?"

After the usual jumping out of her skin, Melissa glanced down and saw Jeremiah grinning away.

"We're at the steel mill," she said in a lowered voice. "The knight is right over there." She held out her wrist so Jeremiah could see for himself.

Jeremiah gulped. "Well, I see by the clock on the wall that it's time to make like a tree and bud."

"You mean *leaf*? Make like a tree and leaf?"

He gave a nervous giggle. "Yeah, that too."

"But you just got here."

"I know, but curiosity killed the 3-D, computer-generated image."

Before Melissa could answer, he was gone. Just like that. She shook her head. What Jeremiah lacked in verbal skills, he definitely did *not* make up for in bravery. But he had a good reason to be frightened. Come to think of it, so did she. What on earth were they doing there?

"Misty?"

She glanced over at Sean. They were much closer to the building now. He pointed to two large fifty-five-gallon drums pushed over and chugging out their contents along the wall. Contents that looked exactly like the trail of gasoline the knight was running to it.

Suddenly she understood. "It's trying to set the mill on fire!"

Sean nodded.

They watched as the knight finished pouring the trail of gas, then set down the can. It reached into a small bag for something. It was hard to tell at that distance, but it looked like a book of—

"Matches!" Melissa whispered. "It's lighting that trail with a match."

"We gotta stop it!"

Before Melissa could answer, her brother swung his bike to the right. He began riding directly toward the knight, shouting and yelling at the top of his lungs.

"HEY, YOU!" he cried. "YOU CAN'T DO THAT! YOU CAN'T DO THAT!"

The knight looked up, startled.

Melissa wasn't crazy about the idea but saw no other choice. She turned her own bike and followed her brother, also shouting. They closed in fast. Thirty yards away. Twenty. Melissa had no idea what they'd do when they arrived. She hoped Sean had a clue . . . but suspected he didn't. Why should things change now?

The knight looked back down at its matches. It was a struggle trying to light one while wearing metal gloves, but at last it dragged it across the striker and it flared up.

Melissa and Sean were ten yards away.

"PUT THAT DOWN!" Sean yelled. "PUT IT DOWN NOW!"

Unfortunately, the knight was only too happy to oblige. It dropped the burning match onto the trail of gasoline.

WHOOOOOSHHH . . .

It lit the trail and started following it toward the fifty-five-gallon drums.

Sean veered to the left, racing to the front of the burning trail. Once there he slammed on his breaks. His back wheel slid around, throwing dirt across the trail and scattering the gasoline. The flame reached the bare spot and came to a stop, still burning but having no place to go.

Melissa watched, impressed.

Unfortunately, the knight wasn't. It turned and quickly stomped toward Sean. But her brother rode away, staying just out of reach.

Good for him . . . not so good for the mill.

As soon as the knight arrived at the bare spot, it poured more gasoline over it. The fire flared up and resumed its course, heading down the trail toward the building.

Sean hopped off his bike and ran a few feet ahead. This time he kicked and scuffed the gas aside with his feet, once again stopping the flame. But he worked so furiously that he didn't see the knight quickly approaching.

"Sean!" Melissa cried. "Sean, look out!"

But Melissa's warning came too late. The knight arrived and lunged for Sean. Its steel claws grabbed the boy's arm. Sean let out a cry and struggled. But it did no good.

The knight had him.

Without thinking, Melissa turned her bike and headed straight for them. Some would call it an act of bravery—she figured it was more like suicide. But that was her brother there. What else could she do?

"Leave him alone!" she shouted as she raced for them. "You leave my broth—"

But that was all she got out before they hit. On the Hunter Catastrophe Scale, it rated an 8.9. It was tremendous, a work of art, destruction at its fine—well, I'll save you the critics' review. Let's just say the air was filled with more flying metal and kids than a carnival ride gone berserk.

When Melissa finally hit the ground, she scrambled to get to her feet. But she'd barely made it to her knees before she felt a cold steel claw grab her arm. She let out a scream and spun around to see *most* of the knight hanging on to her.

"Most" only because, amidst all of the smashing and crashing, the knight had lost his head. Literally. Its helmet had been completely knocked off. And instead of a face, the missing helmet revealed nothing. No face . . . no head . . .

No nothing.

If Melissa had screamed loudly before, she really let loose this time. In fact, it might have been a world record . . . if it hadn't been for her competition. It seems her brother was held in the other claw just as tightly and was busy screaming just as loudly.

But the knight would not let go. Gripping them fiercely, it slowly lumbered to his feet.

10

Checking for Teeth

SUNDAY, 19:02 PDST

"You, Hunters!" The voice bellowed deep within the headless armor. The knight pulled them in closer as they screamed and hollered and fought and struggled. But it did no good. "You have plotted against me, and now you shall pay. Like your ancestors before you, you shall—"

whop-whop-whop-whop

The noise came from behind the steel mill and grew louder by the second.

WHOP-WHOP-WHOP-WHOP

In fact, it grew so loud that it almost drowned out Melissa and Sean's screaming . . . almost. But it was loud enough to distract the knight. He looked up just in time to see a crazy scientist in a lab coat and helicopter tennis shoes appear over their heads.

"It's Doc!" Melissa cried. "Doc is here!"

Suddenly Jeremiah popped back onto Melissa's watch. He was looking up at Doc and shouting orders. "Five degrees port . . . three degrees starboard . . ." And with each order he shouted, Doc drew closer and closer. "Lower . . . lower . . . easy . . ."

The knight was so distracted that Melissa spun away and broke from its grip, but only for a second. It grabbed her again, pulling her in and preparing to . . . preparing to . . . well, she wasn't sure what it was preparing to do, though she figured it probably wouldn't be a lot of fun.

But there was no need to worry. Doc had swooped in close enough to give the knight a good solid kick in the back of the shoulders. It staggered forward.

Doc rose up and dropped down again, giving it another kick . . . and then another.

The knight continued to stumble and stagger until it finally released Melissa and Sean.

They started running . . . past the gas can . . . past the burned-out trail of gas . . . past the pickup . . . past the—

"Hey, wait a minute," Sean yelled. "Wait a minute!"

Melissa slowed to a stop. She leaned over, gasping for breath.

"What are we doing?" he yelled.

"Running for our lives?" she offered.

"No . . . no. We can't catch that knight by running away from it."

"We can't catch it by getting killed, either."

They looked back at the knight, who was still being dive-bombed by Doc.

"We gotta help Doc!" he insisted. "We gotta finish the job! We gotta capture the knight!"

"No way!" Melissa shouted. "We can't catch it! There's no way we can . . ." But she came to a stop. Her brother was no longer listening. He was looking into the back of the pickup . . . at the long piece of coiled rope.

"Absolutely not," she protested. "If you think for one—"

"Misty." He reached for the rope. "If you grab one end and—"

"You can't possibly expect us to—"

"I'll grab the other end—"

"Sean . . ."

"There's no reason why we can't circle around that thing and tie it up."

Melissa shook her head.

"Why not?"

"'Cause I don't like dying, that's why."

"You see how slowly it moves."

"No."

"Misty . . ."

That's when she made her mistake. That's when she looked into his eyes. He was giving her that puppy-dog look—the one he always used when he needed her help. "Doc's over there risking her life for us," he insisted. "We can't desert her."

Against her better judgment, she looked back to where Doc was still dive-bombing the knight. Somehow she knew she'd already lost the argument.

"Everybody's depending on us . . . we can't let them down."

Slowly, she turned back to her brother. He was already holding out the rope to her.

"It's time to face our fears, sis." He gave a half smile, obviously fighting back his own uneasiness. "It's time you and me . . . it's time we both look into that lion's mouth."

Melissa hated it when he was right. Particularly when it meant major bodily damage. But she agreed—it had to be done. Reluctantly, she reached out and took one end of the rope.

"All right!" Sean shouted. "Let's do it!" They turned to face the knight. "Let's bag ourselves a lion!"

The two started running toward the knight, spreading out the rope until it was taut across the ground. When it reached the knight's feet, Sean shouted, "Now, Misty! Start circling now!"

She cut in from the left, and Sean cut in from the right.

At first the knight, who was still preoccupied with the buzzing Doc, didn't understand what they were doing. It wasn't until they'd crossed behind it and started tightening the loop that it realized they were trying to snag it. A problem that it solved by simply stepping over the rope as it passed under its feet.

"We've got to get closer!" Sean yelled. "If we're going to tie it up, we gotta get closer and pull tighter." He moved nearer to the center of the rope and motioned for Melissa to do the same.

She wasn't crazy about getting any closer to the knight but knew her brother was right. If you're going to look into the lion's mouth, you can't do it long distance. She whispered another prayer as she followed Sean's lead, moving up the rope, until she was only a few feet from the dreaded knight.

"Now!" Sean shouted. "Circle around!"

Once again they circled the knight, this time wrapping it around its knees. They passed each other as they completed the first loop.

"Way to go!" Sean yelled. Then in his typical bragging manner he looked back over his shoulder and shouted at the knight. "We got you now, you pile of bolts!"

And they might have had it, too . . . if Sean had done a little more looking and a lot less bragging. But he didn't . . . which meant he didn't see the rock in front of him . . . which meant he tripped over that rock . . . which meant he fell and sprawled out face first onto the ground.

The knight quickly took advantage of the situation, slipping the loop down off its knees and over its feet. Once free, it started toward Sean.

"Look out!" Melissa screamed. "Sean, look out!"

But Sean wasn't moving fast enough, so she reversed directions. Now she was running back at the knight, barely ducking under its swinging arm, then wrapping another loop around it, this time much higher.

Sean rolled away and scrambled to his feet. "Way to go!" he shouted. "Again! Let's do it again!"

Melissa panted for breath as she joined her brother in circling the knight again, so close she could hear the thing gasping for its own breath.

They finished the second loop and went in for a third. If ever they were looking into the lion's mouth, it was now. They were so close they could have touched it.

"Now pull!" Sean shouted.

Before the knight could react, they pulled on the rope, tightening it around its waist and legs. It bent over, trying to free itself, but it was too late. They pulled and it staggered . . . one step, two steps, three . . .

"Pull harder!" Sean shouted. "Pull harder!"

Melissa tugged with everything she had. The rope tightened, completely binding the knight's knees and causing the giant suit of armor to finally topple to the ground with a resounding crash.

But the job wasn't over. They worked fast, circling the knight again and again, making a tangled, knotted web impossible for it to break out of.

Off in the distance, Melissa caught a glimpse of an approaching police car. "How'd they know we were here?" she asked.

Sean looked then and shook his head.

Suddenly little Jeremiah popped back on to her watch and flashed his world-famous grin. "Even us chickens know how to peck out 9–1–1!"

Melissa laughed. "You put in the call?"

He nodded proudly.

"Nice work," she said.

"Thanks, but you know how Doc hates crowds."

Melissa nodded and glanced over at Doc, who was hovering off to the side, nervously watching the police car pull to a stop.

Jeremiah continued, "So it's definitely time for the two of us to make like a tree and molt."

Melissa chuckled. "It's 'leaf.' The saying is, 'Make like a tree and *leaf*.' "

Jeremiah nodded. "Whatever. The point is, we're history. So we'll see ya later, crocodile." And then, just like that, he was gone.

Melissa looked over at Doc. She was already turning around and heading for home.

"All right, guys . . ."

Melissa turned to see the policemen approaching. "We got your call. We'll take it from here." She glanced over at Sean, who was already handing his end of the rope to the other officer.

"Boy, are we glad to see you!" he exclaimed.

"So this is the infamous Sir Richard Falcrest?" the first officer said. He stooped down to the fallen armor for a closer look. "The one who's been doing all the robberies."

Sean took a breath and nodded. "Yes, sir."

"So where's its head?"

The second officer, who had already pulled his revolver from his holster, addressed the knight. "Okay, pal, let's get this suit of armor off and find out how visible the rest of you is."

"Don't shoot!" a frightened voice cried from inside. "I'll take off the armor. I'll do whatever you say, just don't shoot."

Melissa and Sean exchanged glances. Suddenly the fearless ghost didn't sound so fearless.

The first officer reached down and started loosening the breastplate. Even now part of Melissa was afraid that when they opened it up, there would be nothing inside. But when they removed the plate, she saw lying helplessly inside . . . Mr. Jennings, the museum's curator!

"So it was you!" Sean cried. "No wonder. You could get to the suit of armor anytime you wanted." He glanced over at Melissa. "And look, he's so short his head doesn't even stick up above the breastplate."

"Yes, it was me," Jennings snarled. "And I would have pulled it off if you kids hadn't gotten in the way."

"But why?" Melissa asked. "What were you trying to 'pull off'?"

The officers continued unwinding the ropes as Jennings spoke. "My brother Robert owns this steel mill. It's been going broke for years. We planned on burning it down to collect the insurance money."

"But why did you rob all those other places?" Sean asked.

"And try to scare everybody?" Melissa added.

"To divert suspicion. I wanted people to blame the fire on the knight just like they did the robberies . . . as part of his revenge."

Once the ropes were off, the police pulled Jennings

out of the bottom portion of armor. They helped him to his feet and started walking him toward their car.

"But . . ." Sean turned to Melissa and frowned, "if his head only came up to the suit's breastplate, how did he see?"

Melissa stooped down to the armor for a closer look. "Like this," she answered as she stuck her finger through two small holes drilled into the chest. "We couldn't see them when the armor was on display because they were covered up by his shield."

Sean nodded and looked back at Jennings as the police eased him into the backseat of their car. "So . . . not only was our knight not a knight, but he wasn't invisible, either."

Melissa nodded, still staring at the fallen armor. "It's just like Dad said . . . this was just another roaring lion without any teeth."

The police shut the back car door, and the first officer called over to them, "Can you kids drop by the station tomorrow? We need to do a little more talking."

"Yes, sir," Sean answered, "we'll be there."

"And I'd be getting home if I were you," the second officer said. "It's getting pretty dark."

"Yes, sir," Melissa replied. "We just need to drop by our dad's station first . . . then we'll be on our way."

The officer nodded as he climbed into the car. But before shutting the door, he added, "Oh, and kids?"

"Yes, sir?" Sean and Melissa both answered.

He broke into a gentle grin. "Nice work."

Epilogue

SUNDAY, 20:09 PDST

"And that's all there is to report on the national scene," Mr. Hunter said, speaking into the microphone. "And in local news—" He suddenly came to a stop as Herbie entered the broadcast booth, waving a note.

"Excuse me . . . I've just been handed an important bulletin."

He quickly scanned the note, and his eyes widened. Then he cleared his throat and continued. "In local news, police have a suspect in the recent invisible knight robberies. Edgar Jennings, curator of the Middleton Museum, was arrested only a half hour ago as he attempted to set fire to the Pierce and Jennings Steel Mill. He was wearing a suit of armor taken from the museum. Police were assisted in the capture by two agents from

. . . the Bloodhounds, Inc. Detective Agency."

Mr. Hunter set the note down and continued speaking into the mike. "That's the news in Middelton. My name is Robert Hunter, and those detectives you just heard about? They're my children, Sean and Melissa. Now it's back to music with 101 harmonicas playing *Ode to Joy* from Beethoven's Ninth Symphony."

The music started, and Mr. Hunter was out of the broadcast booth in a flash. "Herbie, what is all this about?"

The engineer shrugged and nodded toward the lunchroom, where Melissa and Sean sat, eagerly waiting.

"Hey, Dad," Melissa grinned.

"Hope you didn't mind us writing the news bulletin," Sean added, "but we figured you should have the first scoop."

Dad pulled up a chair and straddled it. "Let me get this straight. You two solved the case of the invisible knight?"

They nodded enthusiastically.

He shook his head in wonder. "That's amazing. . . ."

"All we did was practice what you preached," Melissa said.

Dad looked at her.

"You said with God on our side, we had nothing to fear."

Sean added, "So we looked the lion in the mouth, and you were right. . . ."

"I was?"

"Yup," Melissa grinned. "When we got close enough to it, we saw that it didn't have any teeth."

Dad stared at Sean, then Melissa, then back at Sean again. They couldn't be sure, but it almost looked like he was starting to tear up.

"Dad . . ." Melissa asked, "are you all right?"

He wiped his eyes and glanced away. "Yeah . . . uh . . ." Then he looked back up. "I'm just really proud of you guys. Not only for solving the case . . . but for having that type of faith."

"All in a day's work," Sean said, clasping his hands behind his head and looking anything but humble.

"Oh." Dad reached into his pocket to pull out a piece of paper. "I got this note from Dr. Troast."

Melissa felt her throat tighten, wondering what news the veterinarian had.

Dad grinned. "It sounds like Slobs is going to make it. She'll be home in just a few days."

"All right!" Sean and Melissa high-fived.

Dad rose from his chair. "Listen, I'm just wrapping up here. Why don't you load your bikes into the van, and I'll take you home."

"Deal," Sean said.

"Sounds good to me," Melissa added.

With that they rose and headed toward the door. Unfortunately, this was exactly the same door Herbie was entering with another one of his famous ham, tuna, cheese, dill pickle, and whatever-else-was-left-in-the-station's-refrigerator sandwiches.

Well, he *had* been entering with the sandwich. Now he was busy watching it sail through the air. Everyone looked on with awe as it hit the broadcast window with a splat and slowly oozed down the glass.

For a moment there was dead silence. Then someone snickered, then someone else, until finally everyone in the room broke out laughing. Even Herbie. Because as nice as it was to know that we don't have to be afraid with God on our side, it was also good to see that some things in life never really change. . . .

By Bill Myers

Children's Series:
Bloodhounds, Inc. — mystery/comedy
Journeys to Fayrah — fantasy/allegorical
McGee and Me! — book and video
The Incredible Worlds of Wally McDoogle — comedy

Teen Series:
Forbidden Doors

Adult Novels:
Blood of Heaven
Threshold
Fire of Heaven

Nonfiction:
Christ B.C.
The Dark Side of the Supernatural
Hot Topics, Tough Questions

Series for Middle Graders*
From Bethany House Publishers

ADVENTURES DOWN UNDER · by Robert Elmer
When Patrick McWaid's father is unjustly sent to Australia as a prisoner in 1867, the rest of the family follows, uncovering action-packed mystery along the way.

ADVENTURES OF THE NORTHWOODS · by Lois Walfrid Johnson
Kate O'Connell and her stepbrother Anders encounter mystery and adventure in northwest Wisconsin near the turn of the century.

AN AMERICAN ADVENTURE SERIES · by Lee Roddy
Hildy Corrigan and her family must overcome danger and hardship during the Great Depression as they search for a "forever home."

BLOODHOUNDS, INC. · by Bill Myers
Hilarious, hair-raising suspense follows brother-and-sister detectives Sean and Melissa Hunter in these madcap mysteries with a message.

JOURNEYS TO FAYRAH · by Bill Myers
Join Denise, Nathan, and Josh on amazing journeys as they discover the wonders and lessons of the mystical Kingdom of Fayrah.

MANDIE BOOKS · by Lois Gladys Leppard
With over four million sold, the turn-of-the-century adventures of Mandie and her many friends will keep readers eager for more.

THE RIVERBOAT ADVENTURES · by Lois Walfrid Johnson
Libby Norstad and her friend Caleb face the challenges and risks of working with the Underground Railroad during the mid–1800s.

TRAILBLAZER BOOKS · by Dave and Neta Jackson
Follow the exciting lives of real-life Christian heroes through the eyes of child characters as they share their faith and God's love with others around the world.

THE TWELVE CANDLES CLUB · by Elaine L. Schulte
When four twelve-year-old girls set up a business doing odd jobs and baby-sitting, they find themselves in the midst of wacky adventures and hilarious surprises.

THE YOUNG UNDERGROUND · by Robert Elmer
Peter and Elise Andersen's plots to protect their friends and themselves from Nazi soldiers in World War II Denmark guarantee fast-paced action and suspenseful reads.

*(ages 8–13)

9706